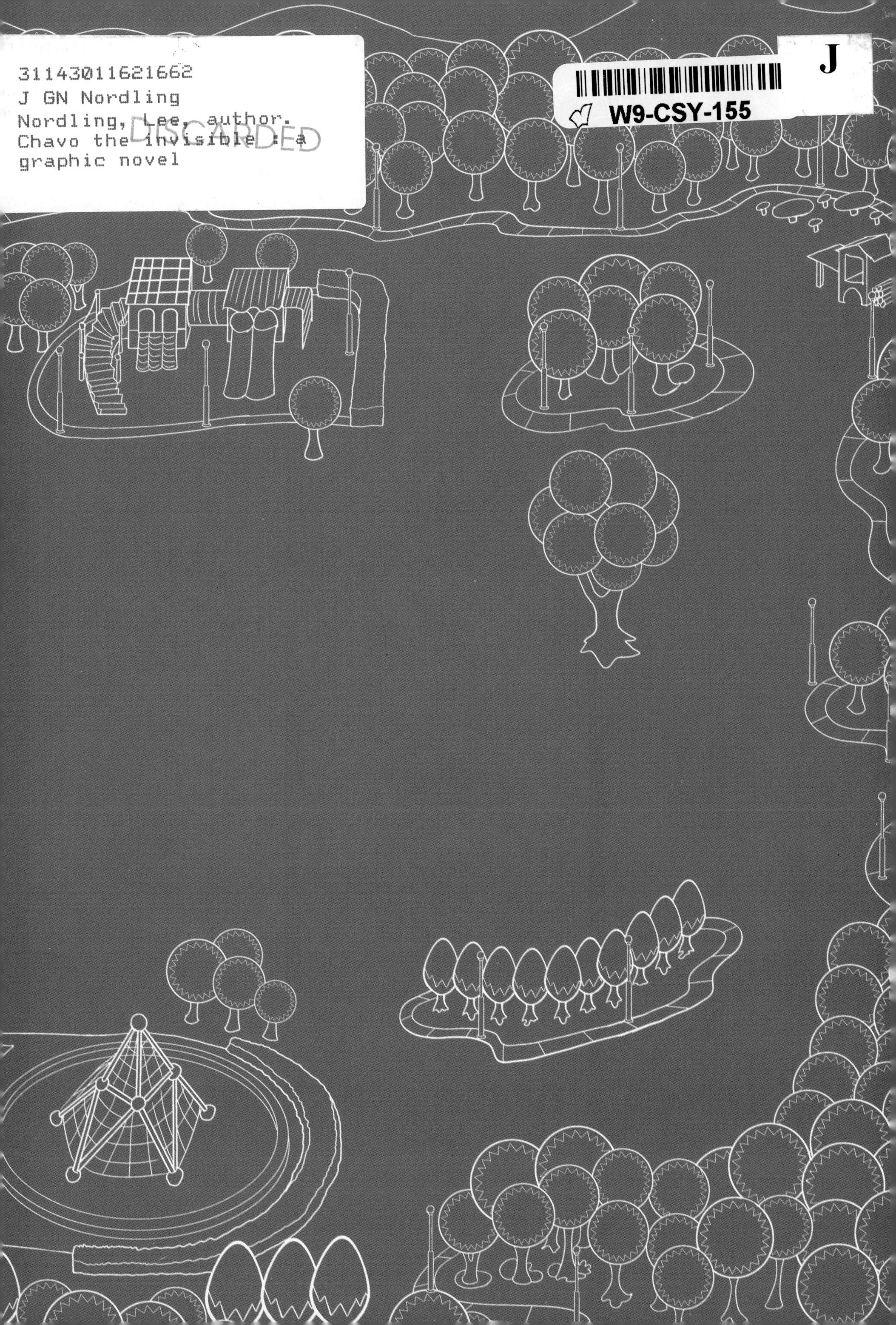

Game for ADVENTURE
Chavo the Invisible

A GRAPHIC NOVEL
Lee Nordling & Flávio Silva

Graphic Universe™ • Minneapolis

For Cheri,
still and forever (which is a really long time)
the love of all of my lives.
And a special thanks to Fabricio Grellet, Greg Hunter, and Danielle Carnito
for helping to shepherd our vision for this story.

– Lee Nordling

Thanks to the entire creative team for this opportunity,
as well as for their help in bringing the visual storytelling to life.
The success of this book is due to the perseverance of this team. Thanks to all!

– Flávio B. Silva

Lee Nordling is a two-time Eisner Award nominee
and award-winning writer, editor, creative director,
and book packager. He worked on staff at
Disney Publishing, DC Comics, and
Nickelodeon Magazine.

Flávio B. Silva is an illustrator, graphic designer, and comic book
artist based in Brazil. Through Magic Eye Studios, he's worked for
comics publishers in the United States and Europe, most notably
for Disney Publishing, DC Comics, and Boom Studios.

Story and script by Lee Nordling
Art by Flávio B. Silva/Magic Eye Studios

Chavo the Invisible © 2018 by Lee Nordling

Chavo the Invisible and the *Game for Adventure* series
were placed, designed, and produced by The Pack.

Graphic Universe™ is a trademark of Lerner Publishing
Group, Inc.

Graphic Universe™
A division of Lerner Publishing Group, Inc.
241 First Avenue North
Minneapolis, MN 55401 USA

For reading levels and more information, look up this title
at www.lernerbooks.com.

Library of Congress Cataloging-in-Publication Data

Names: Nordling, Lee, author. | Silva, Flávio B., illustrator.
Title: Chavo the invisible / written by Lee Nordling ;
    illustrated by Flávio B. Silva.
Description: Minneapolis : Graphic Universe, [2018] |
    Series: Game for adventure | Summary: "A game
    of capture the flag takes a fantastical turn, and one
    participant becomes an unlikely hero" –Provided by
    publisher.
Identifiers: LCCN 2017006470 (print) | LCCN 2017033757
    (ebook) | ISBN 9781512413328 (lb : alk. paper) | ISBN
    9781512498561 (eb pdf) | ISBN 9781541510463 (pbk.)
Subjects: LCSH: Graphic novels. | CYAC: Graphic novels. |
    Tag games–Fiction. | Games–Fiction. | Ability–Fiction. |
    Stories without words.
Classification: LCC PZ7.7.N67 Ch 2018 (print) | LCC
    PZ7.7.N67 (ebook) | DDC 741.5/973–dc23

LC record available at https://lccn.loc.gov/2017006470

Manufactured in the United States of America
1-39790-21327-9/18/2017

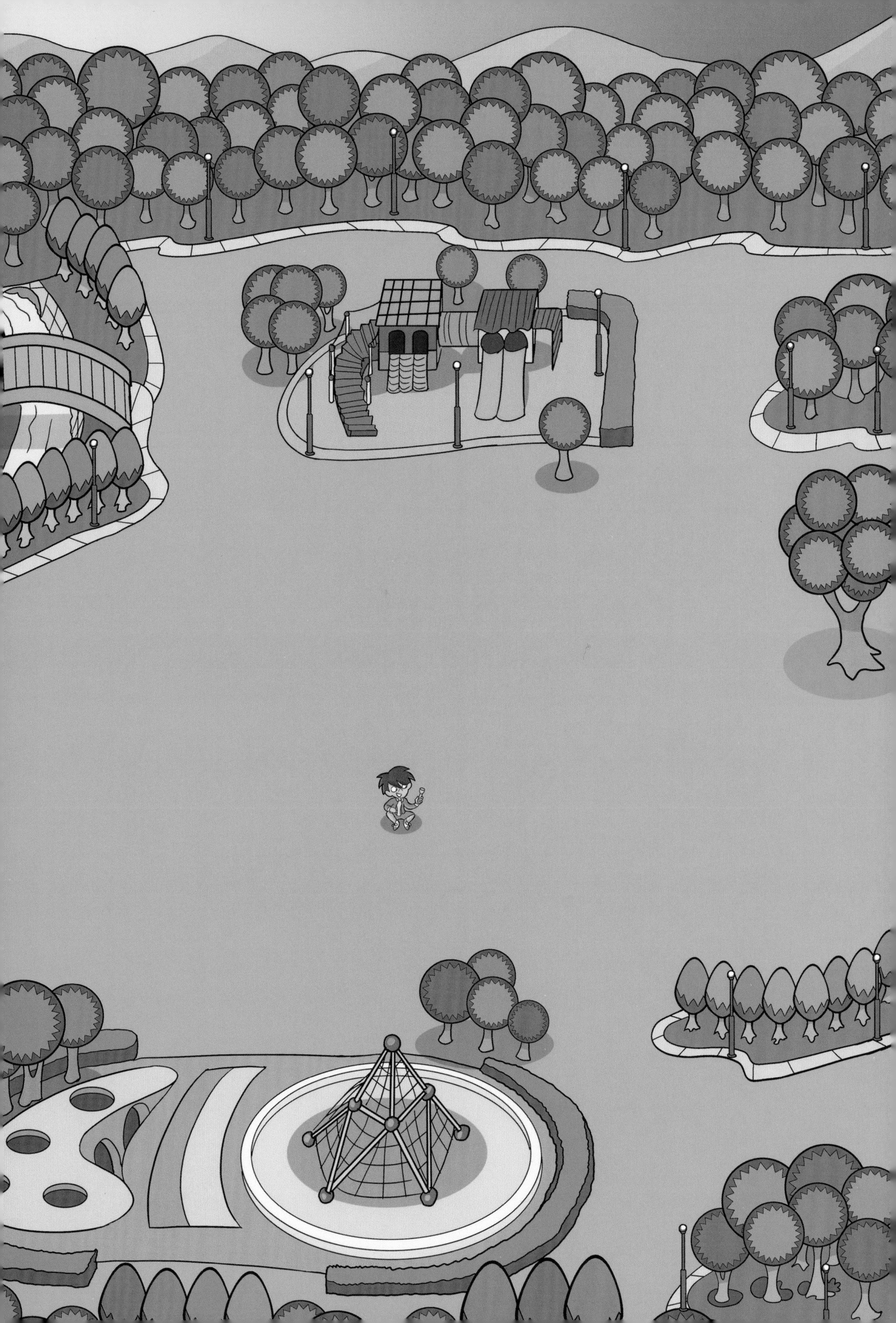

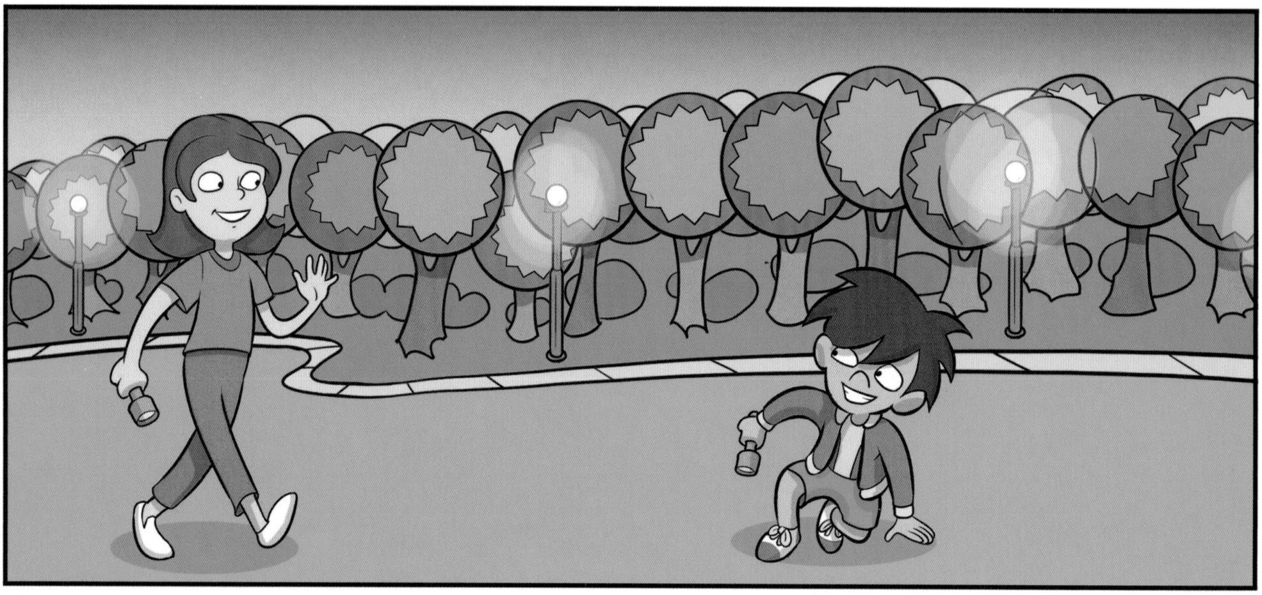

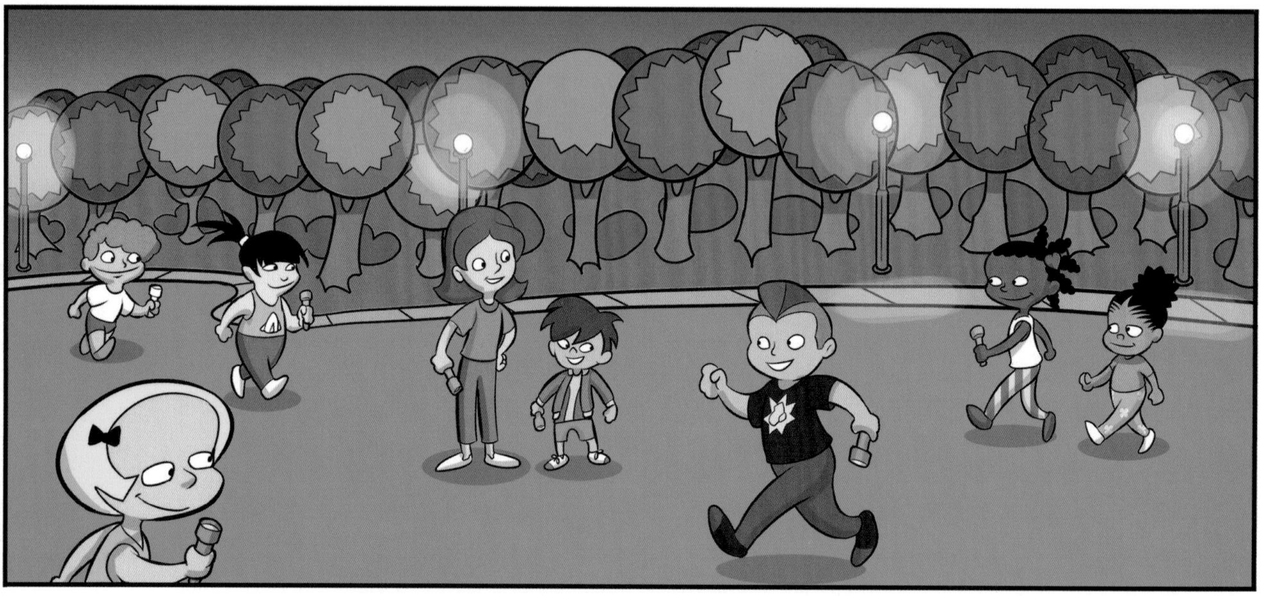

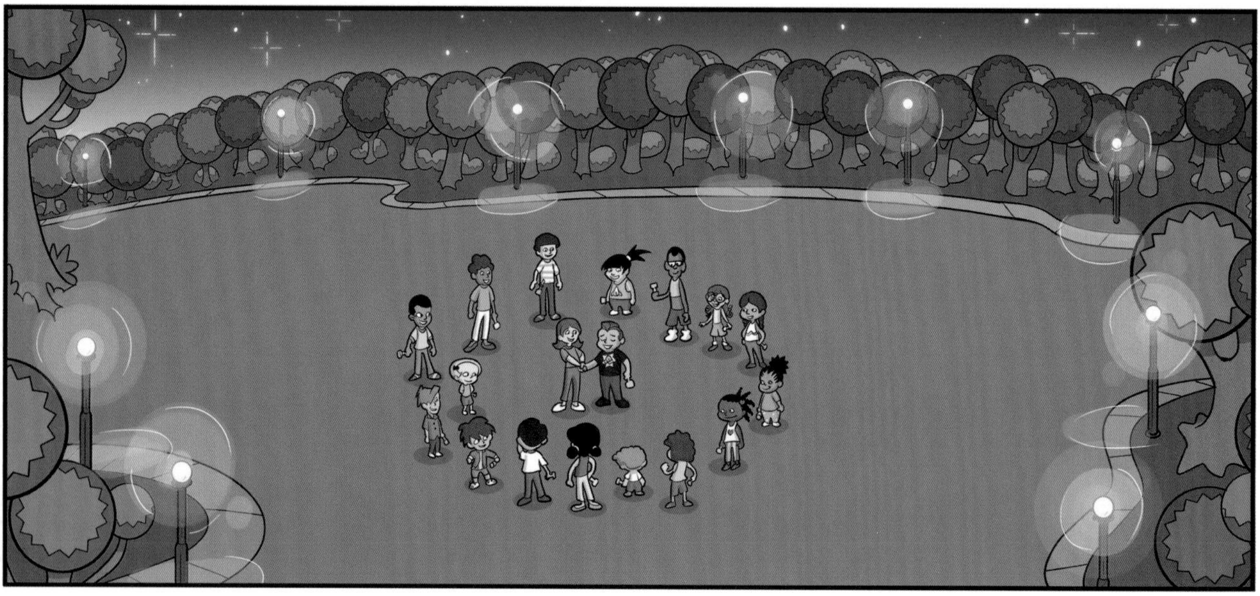

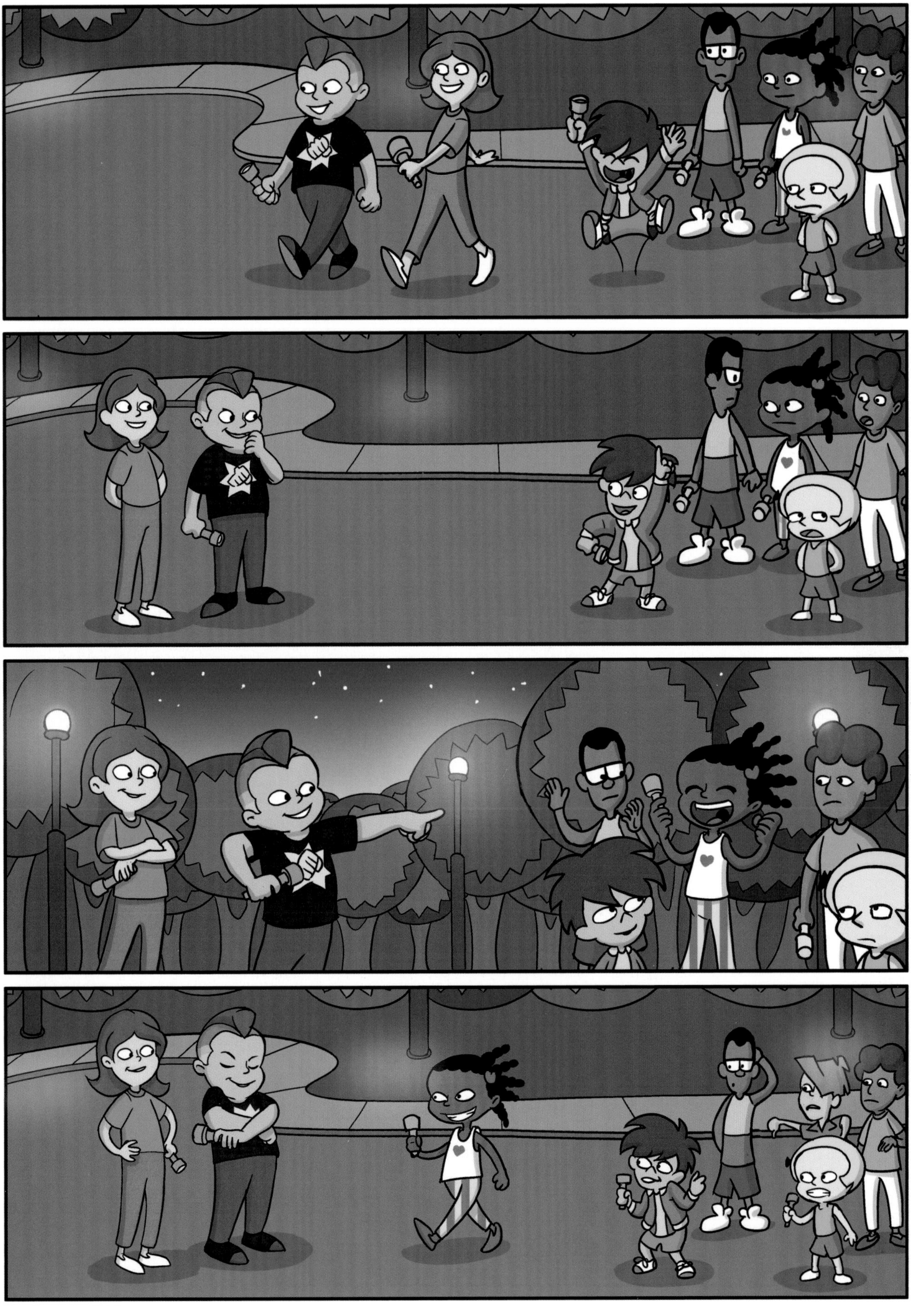

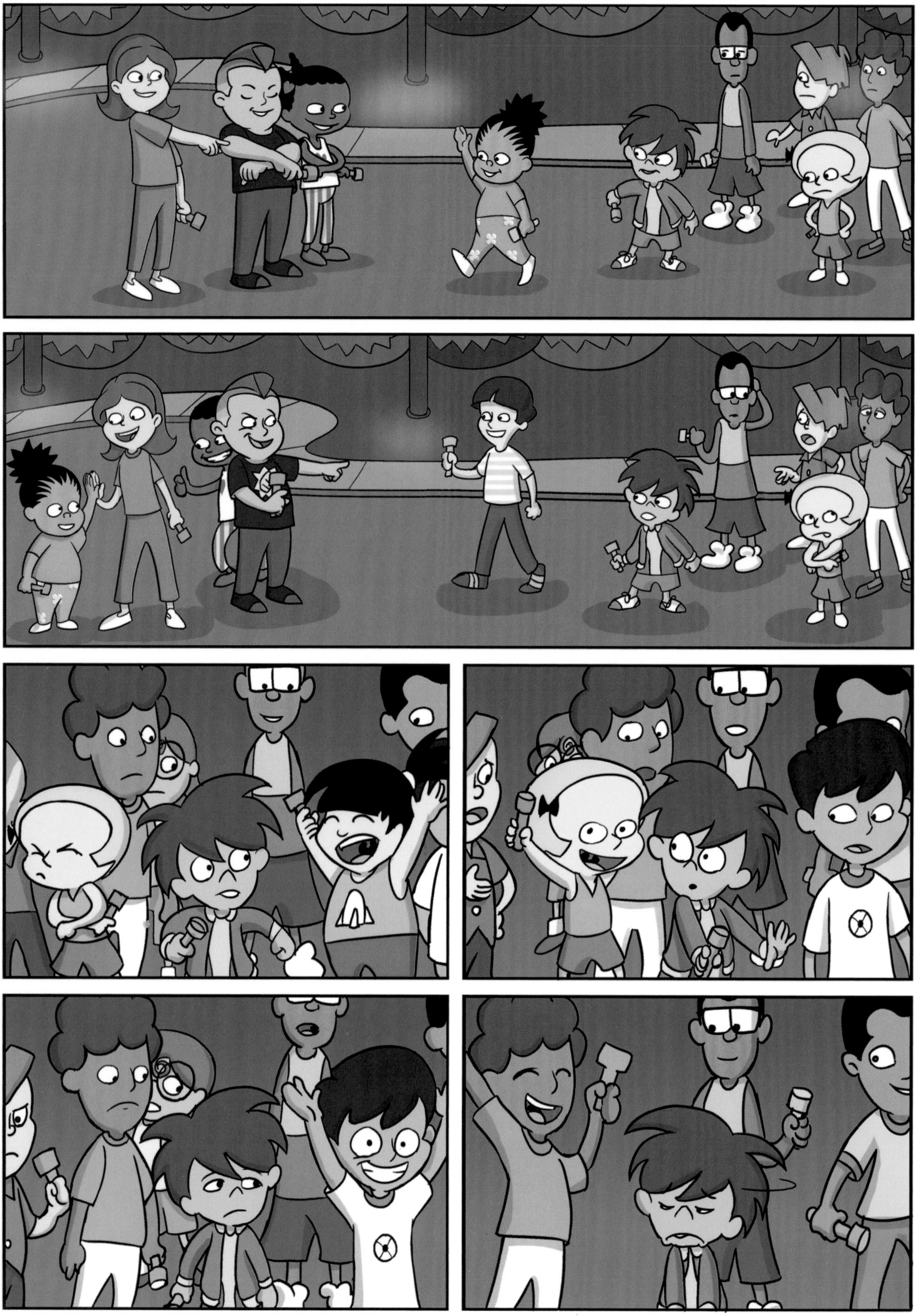

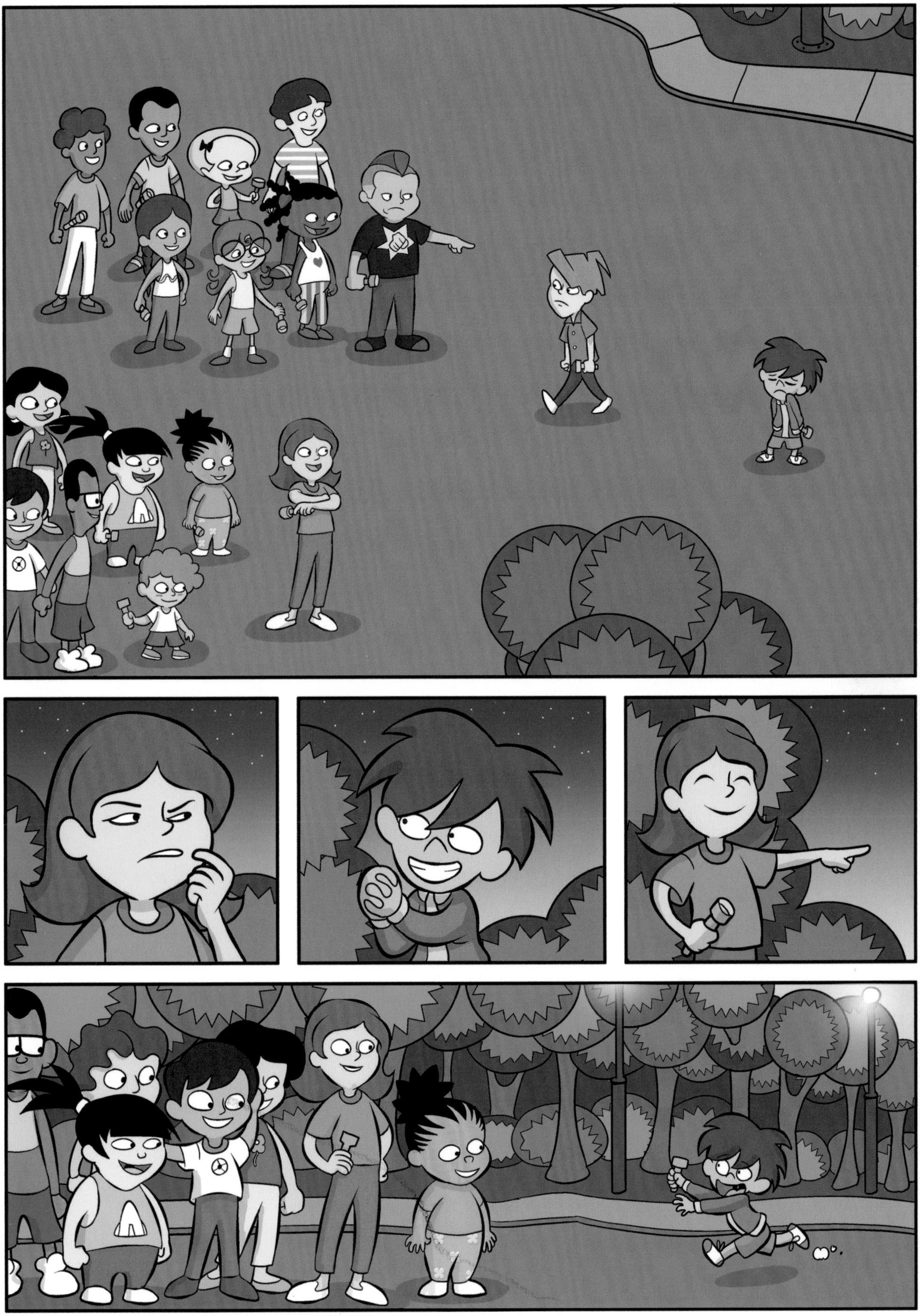

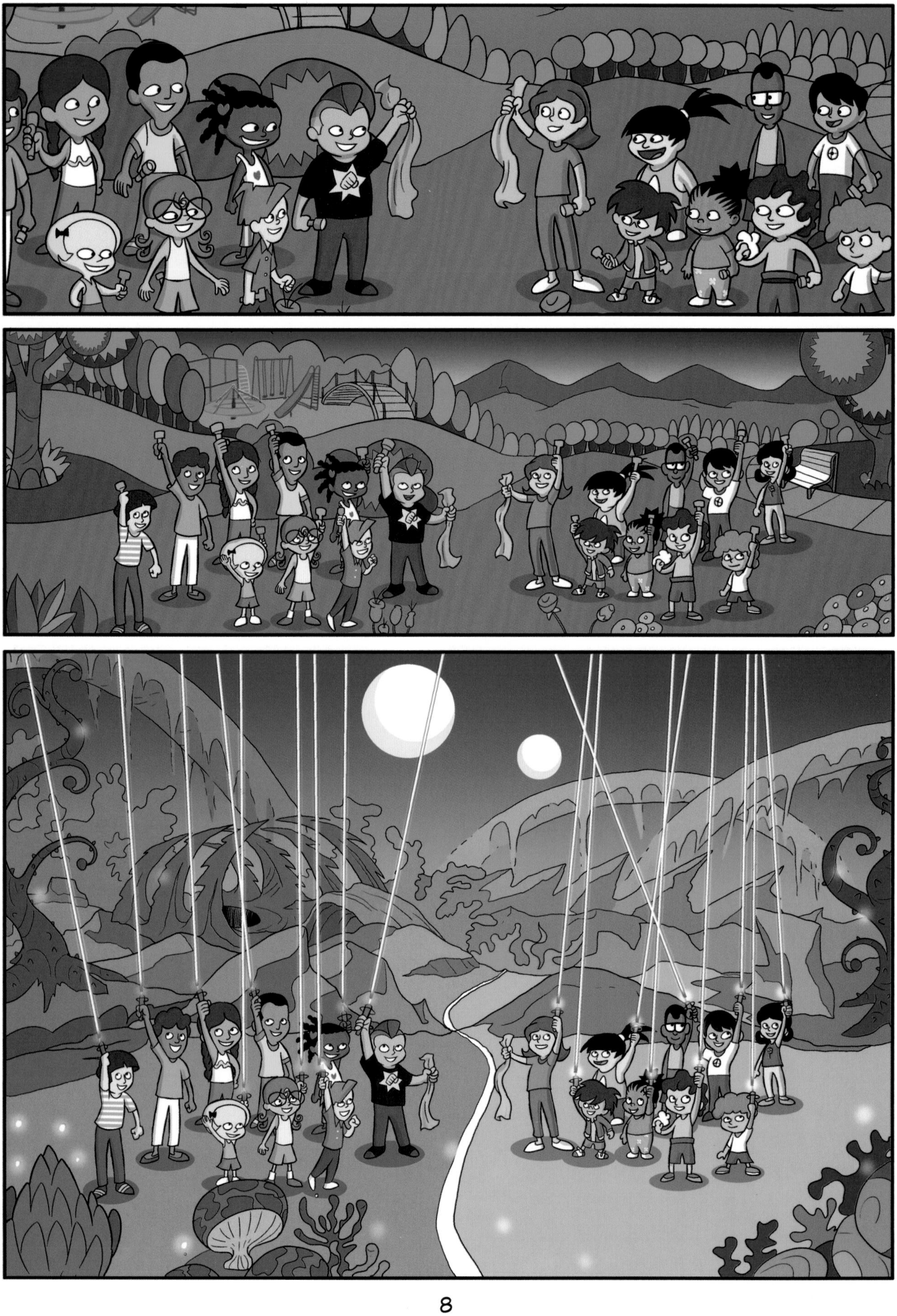

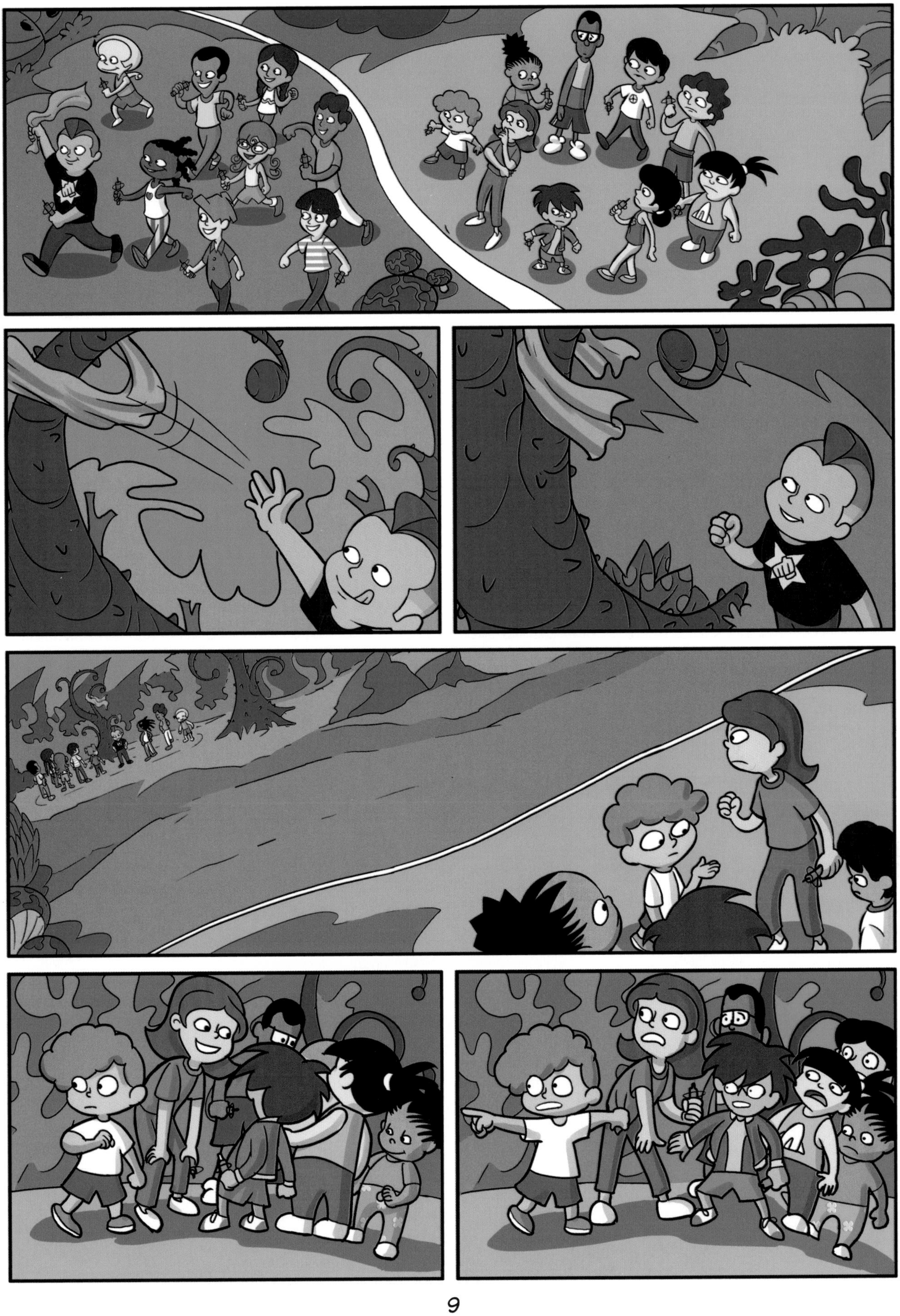

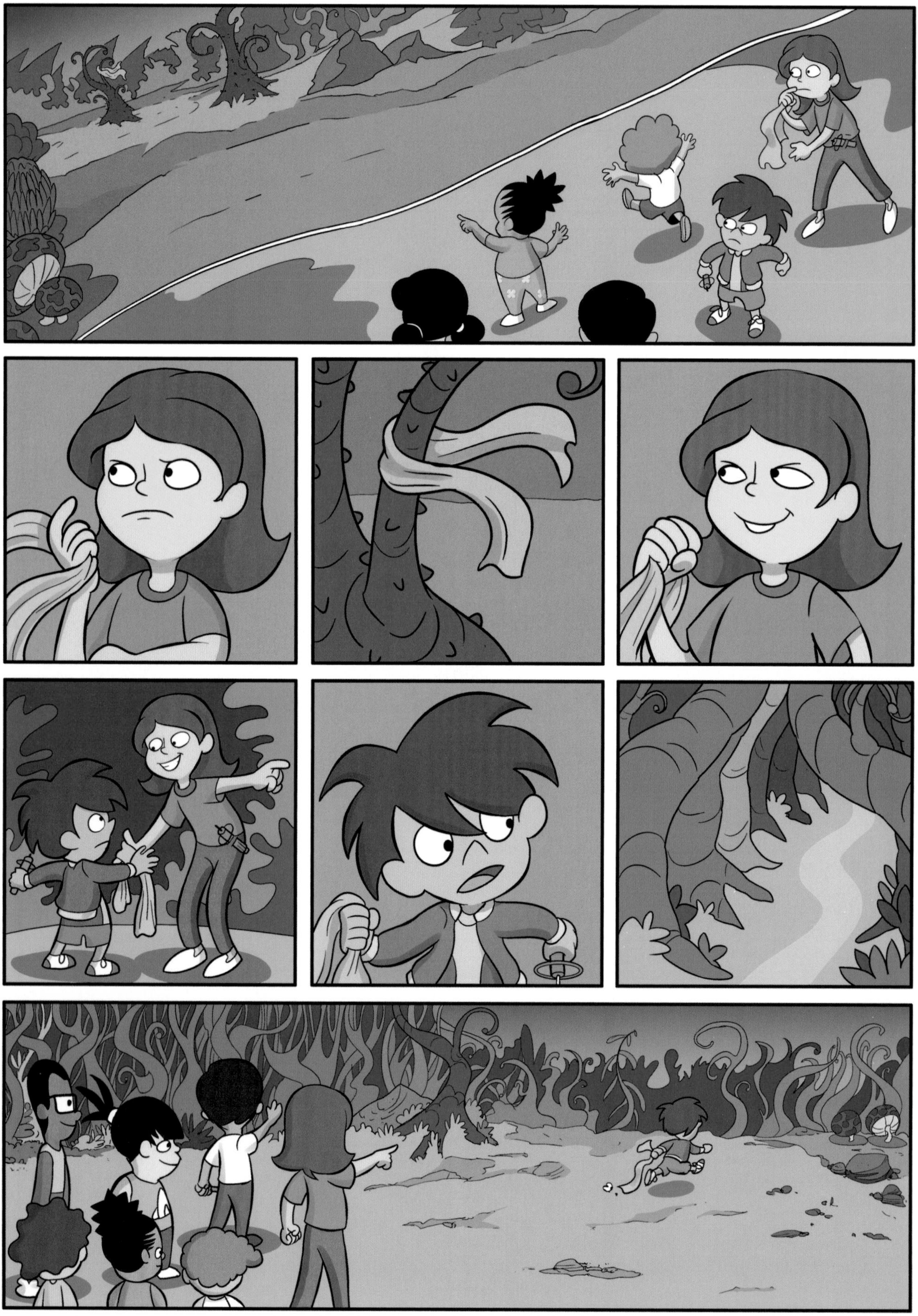

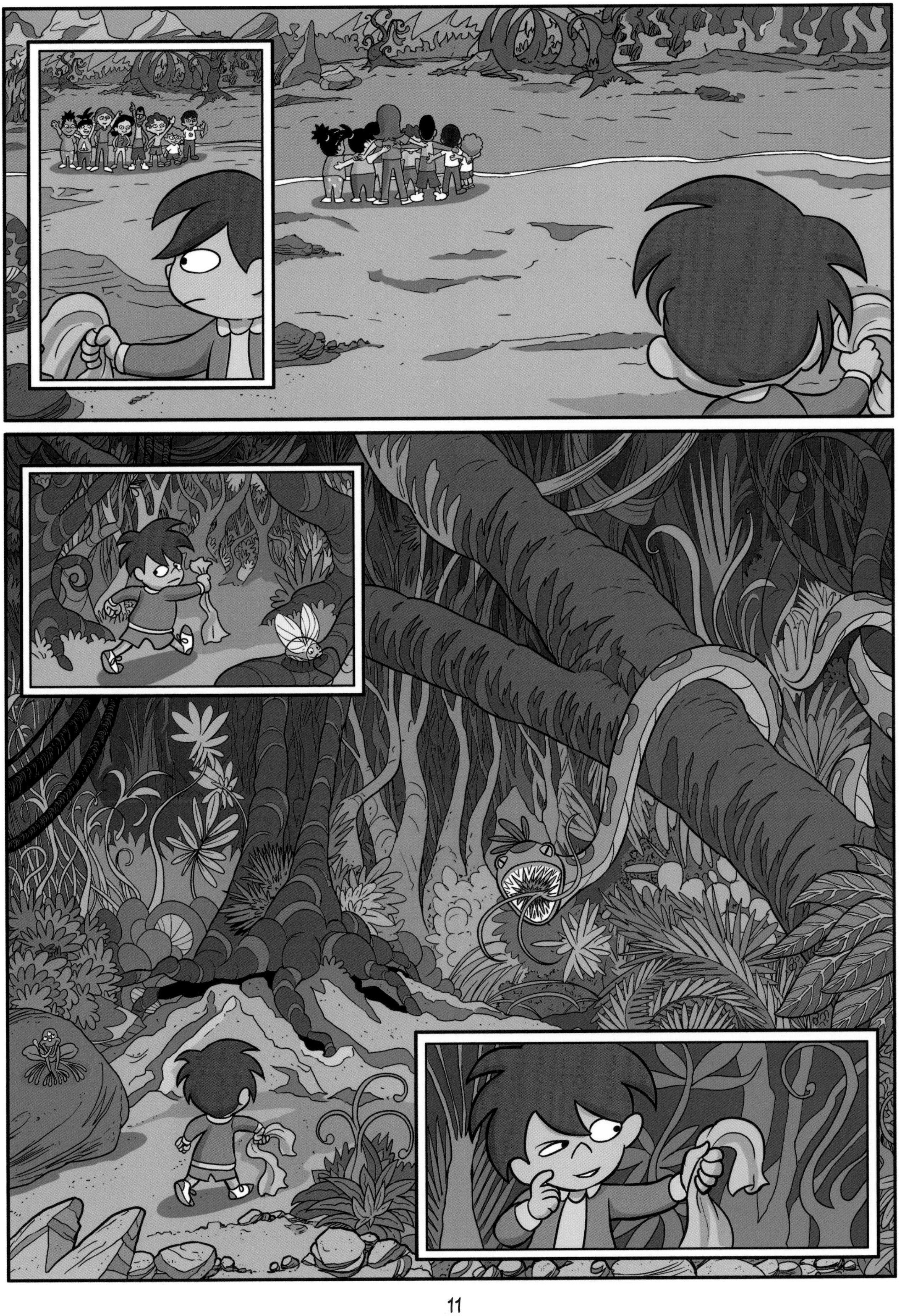

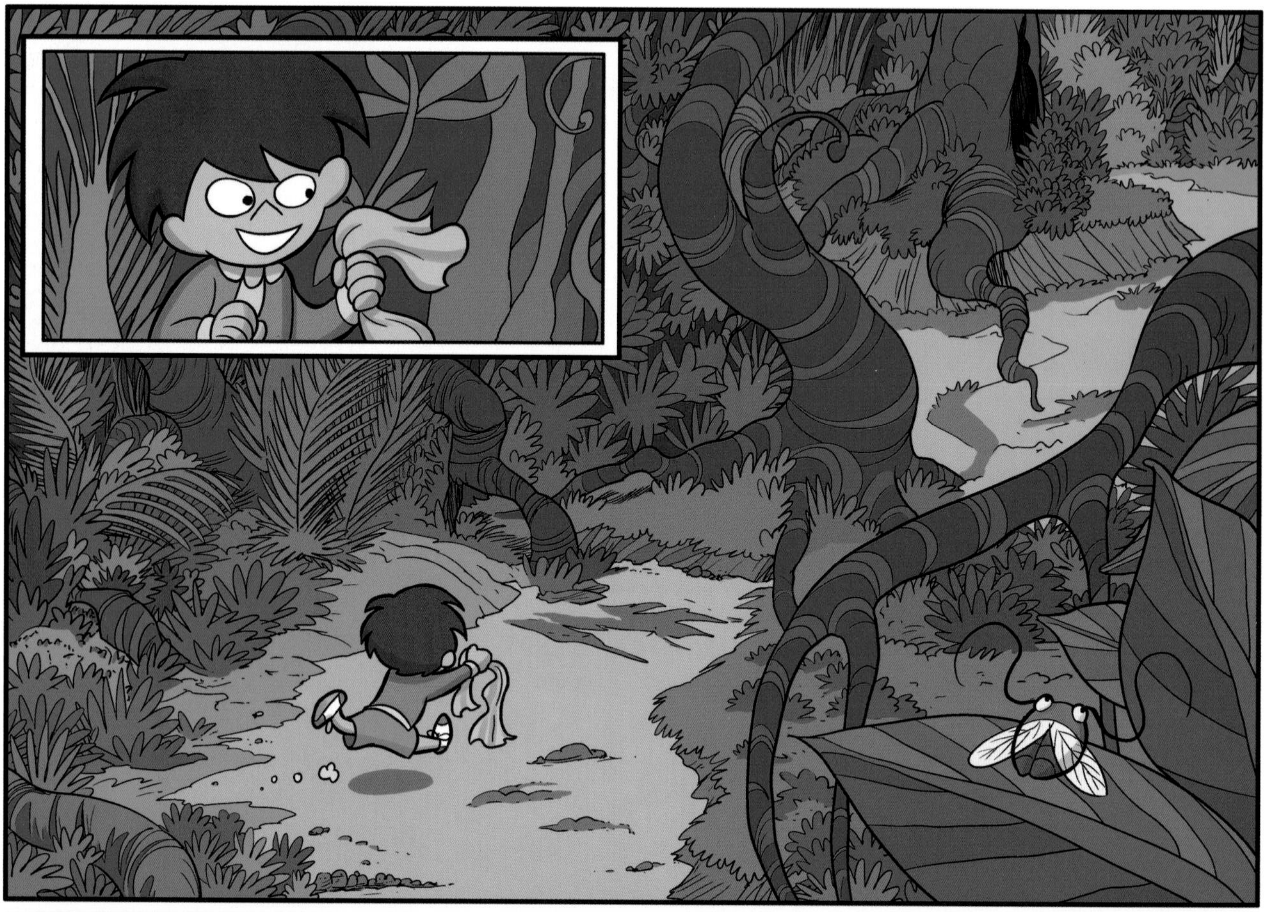

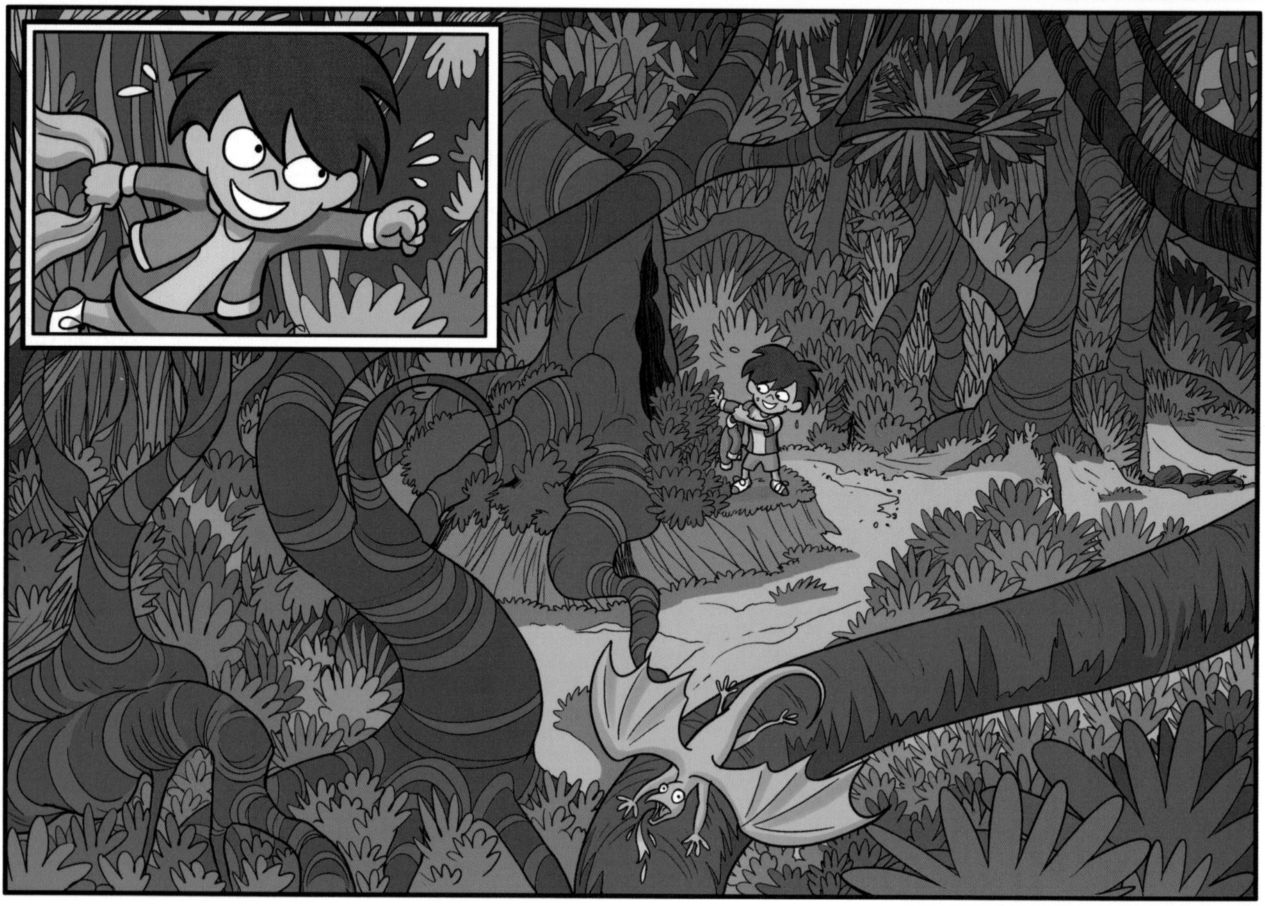

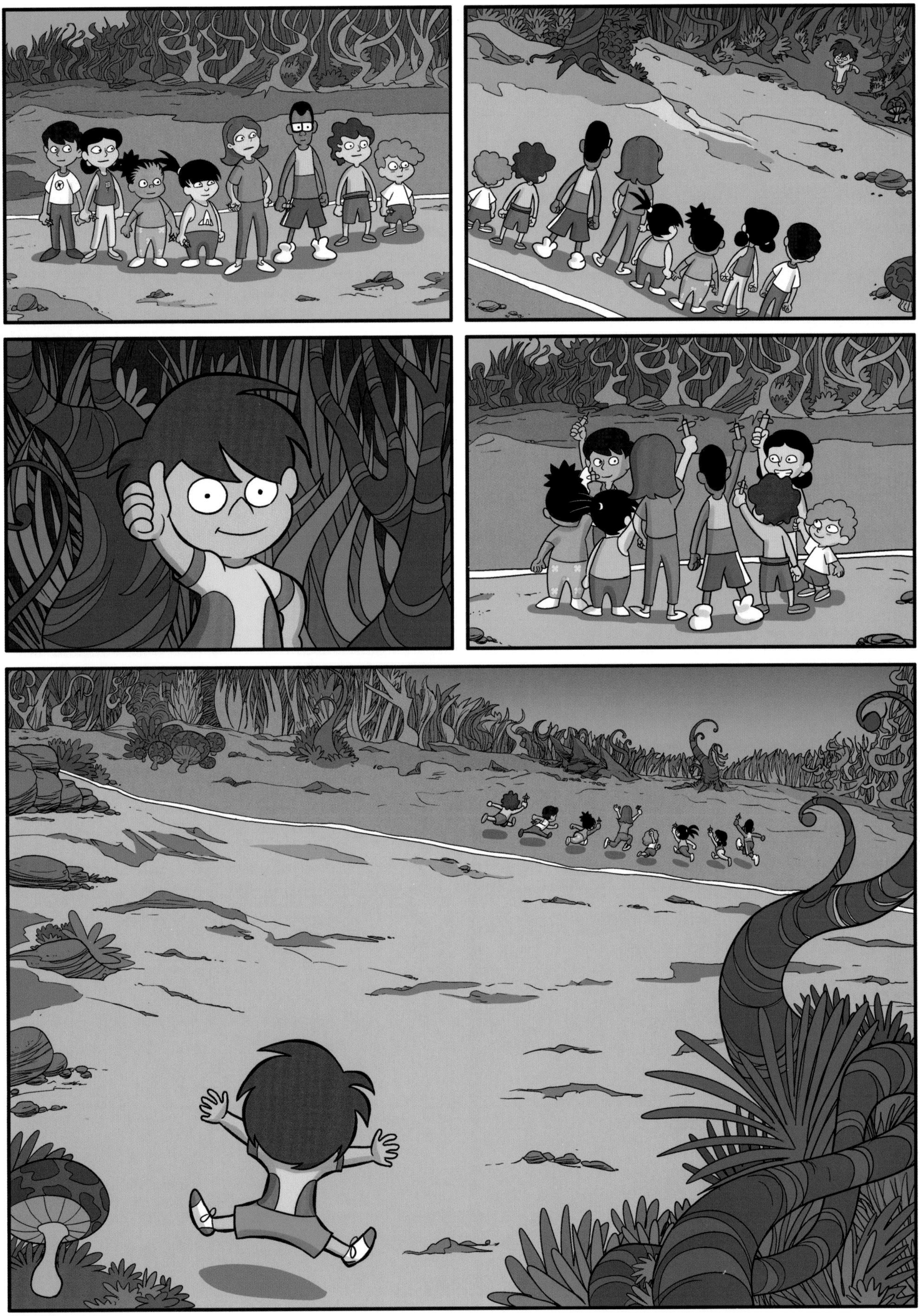

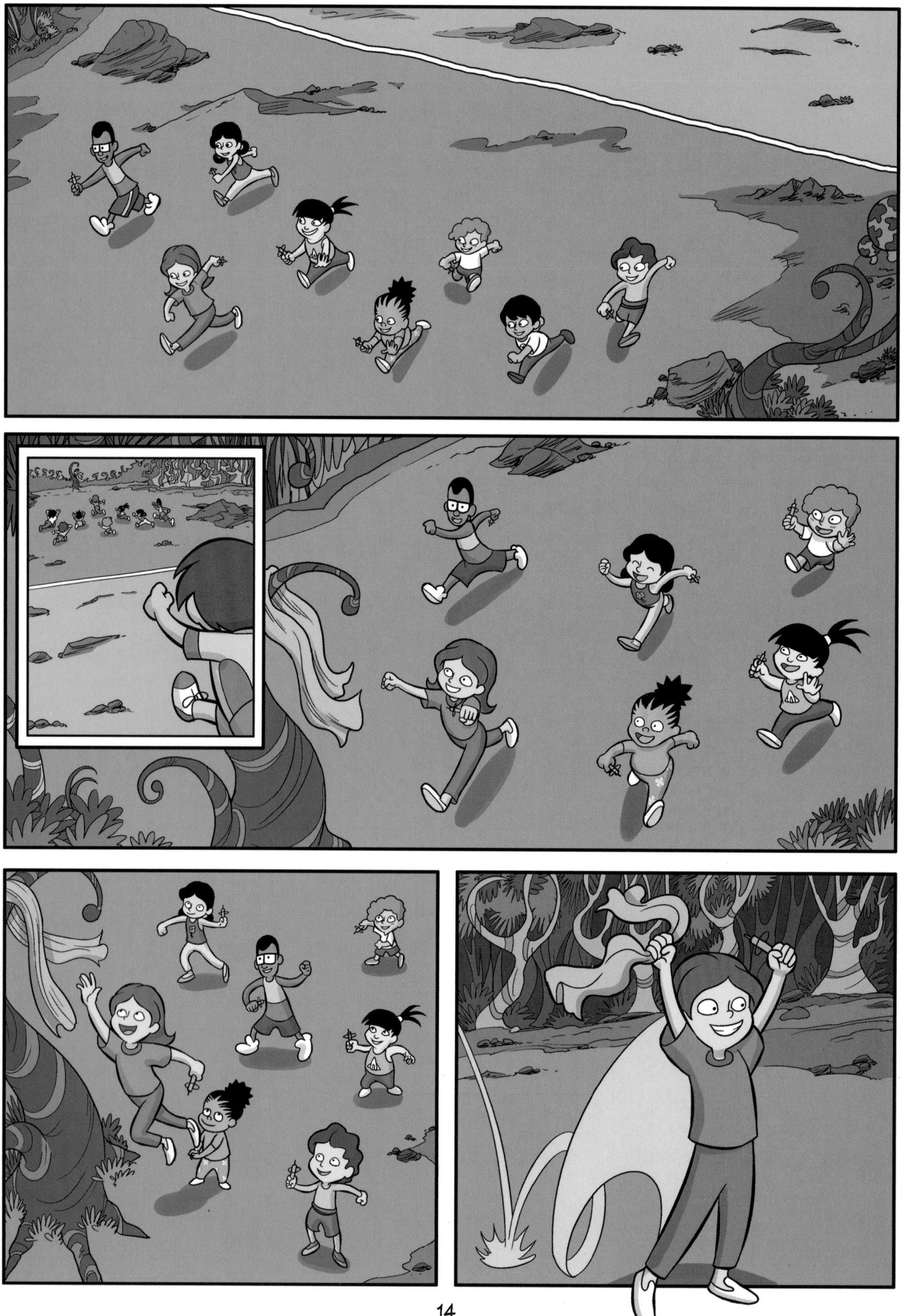

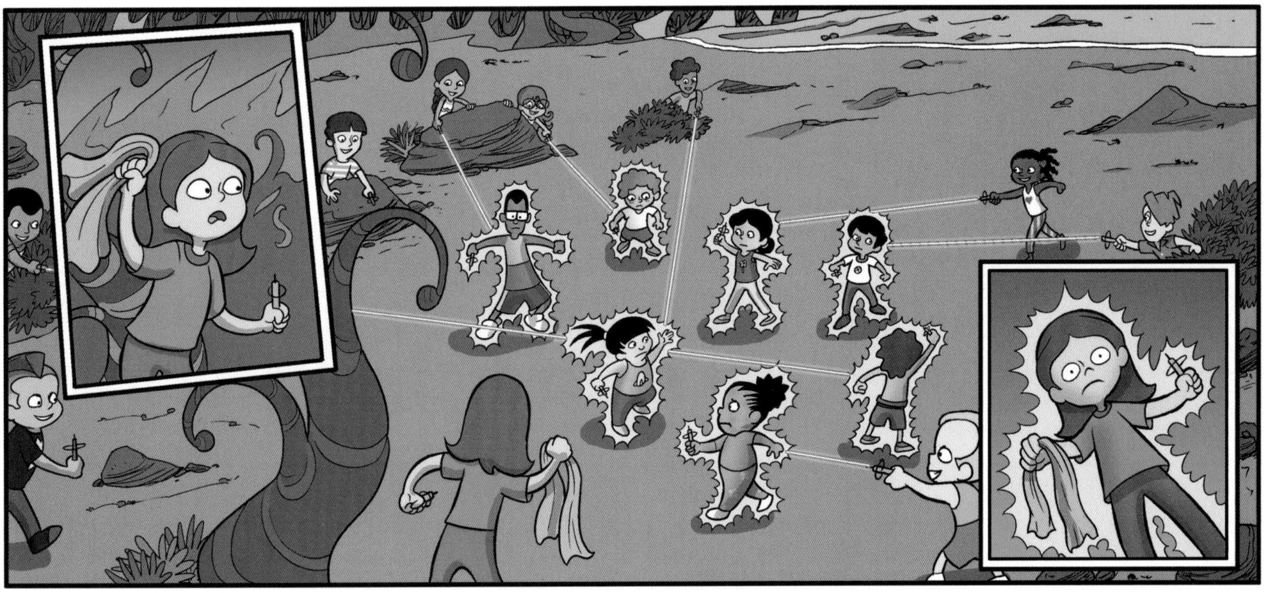

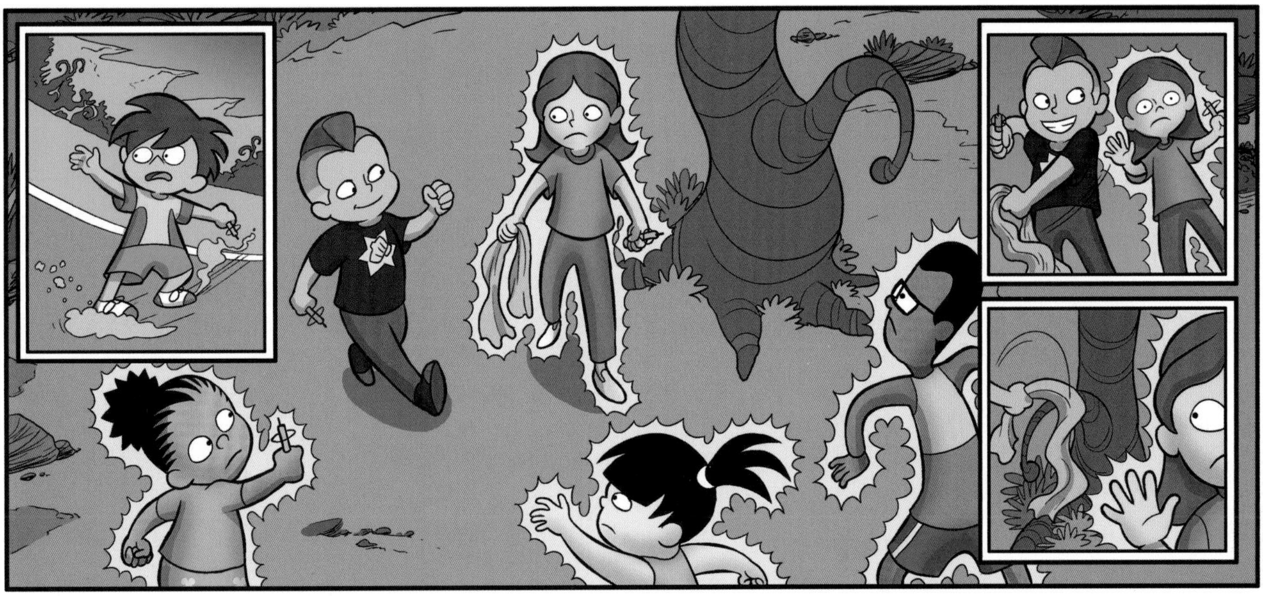

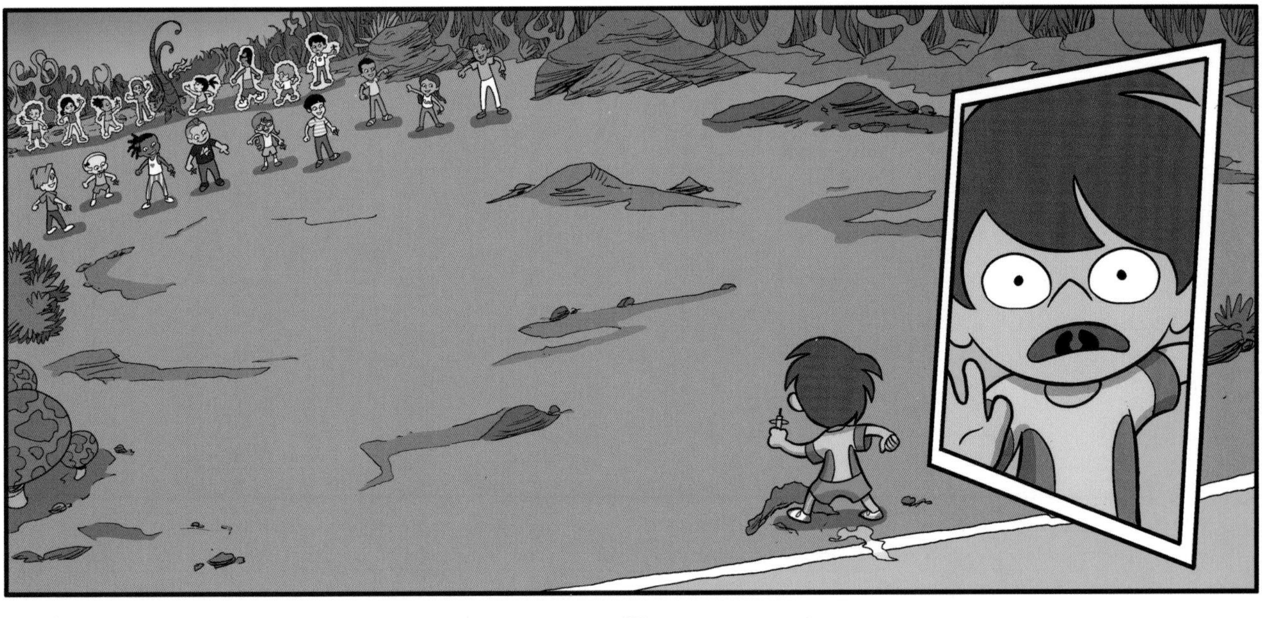

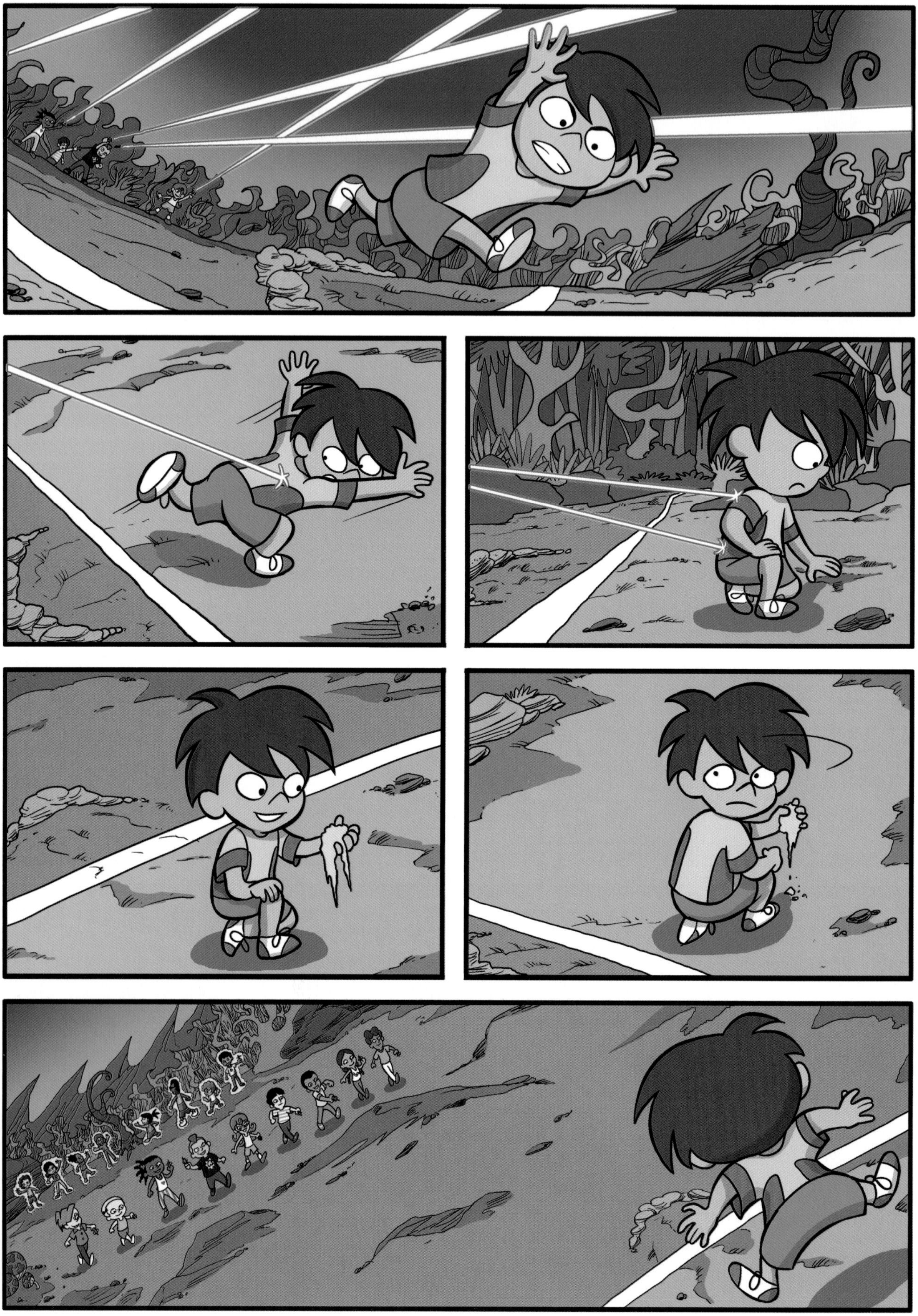

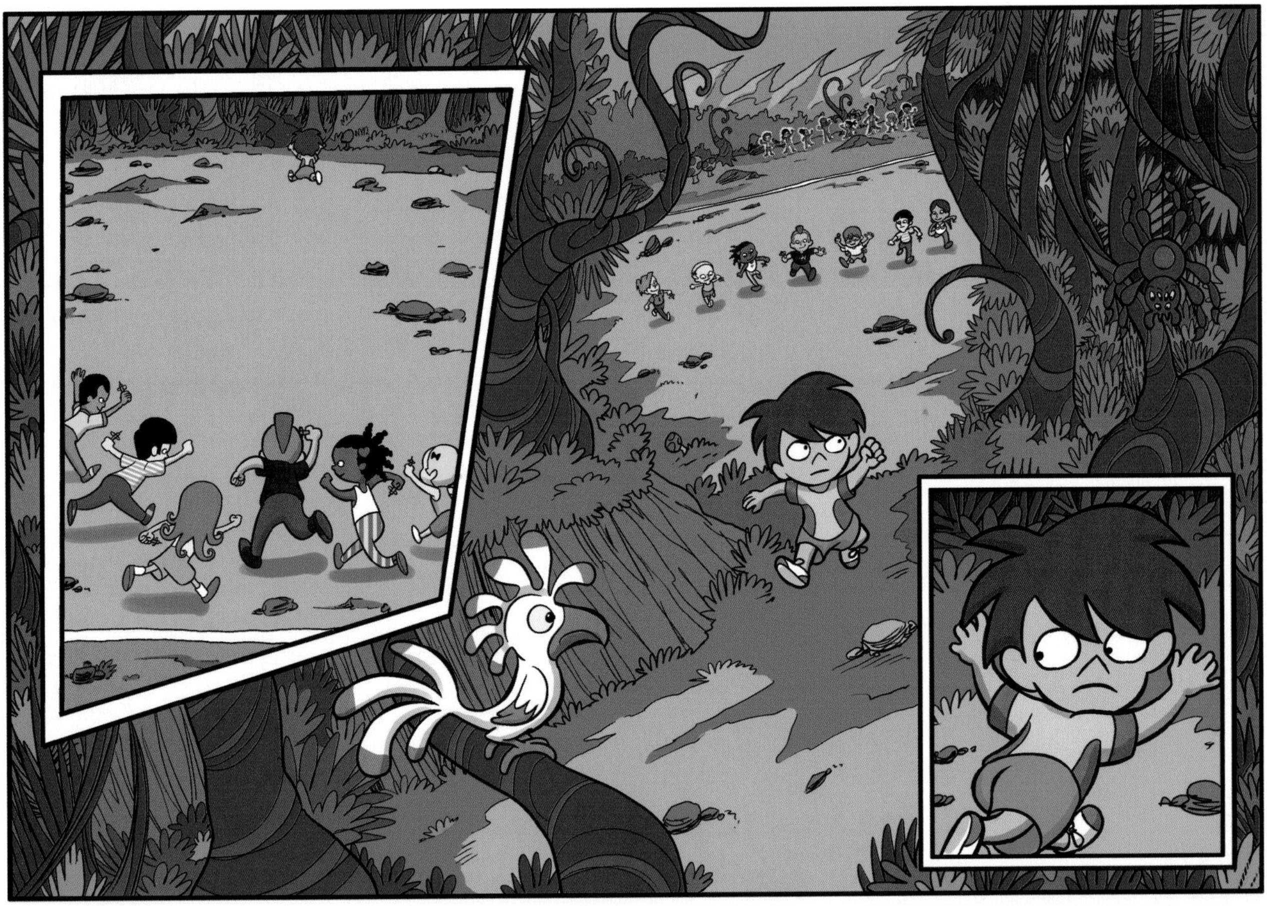

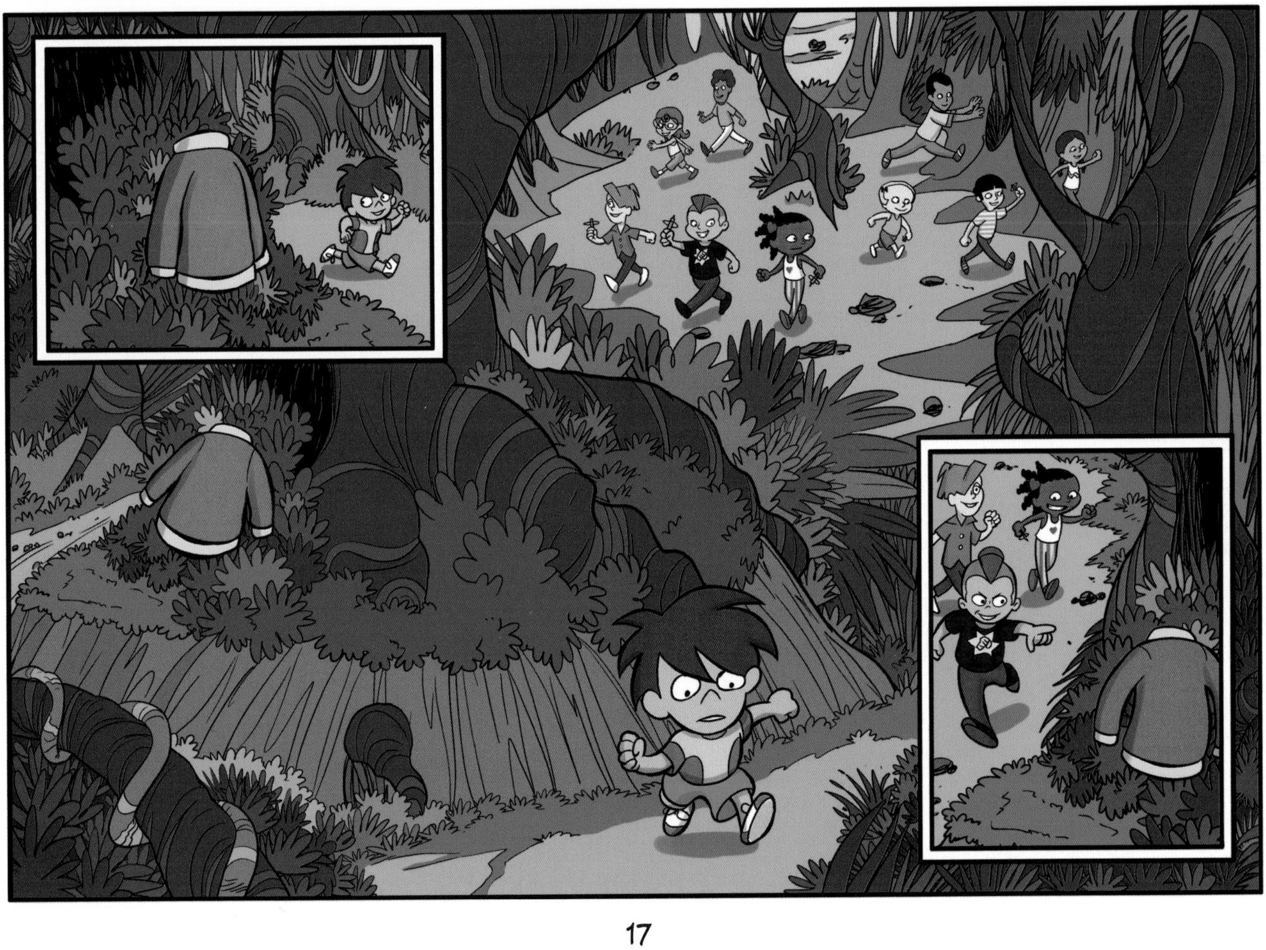

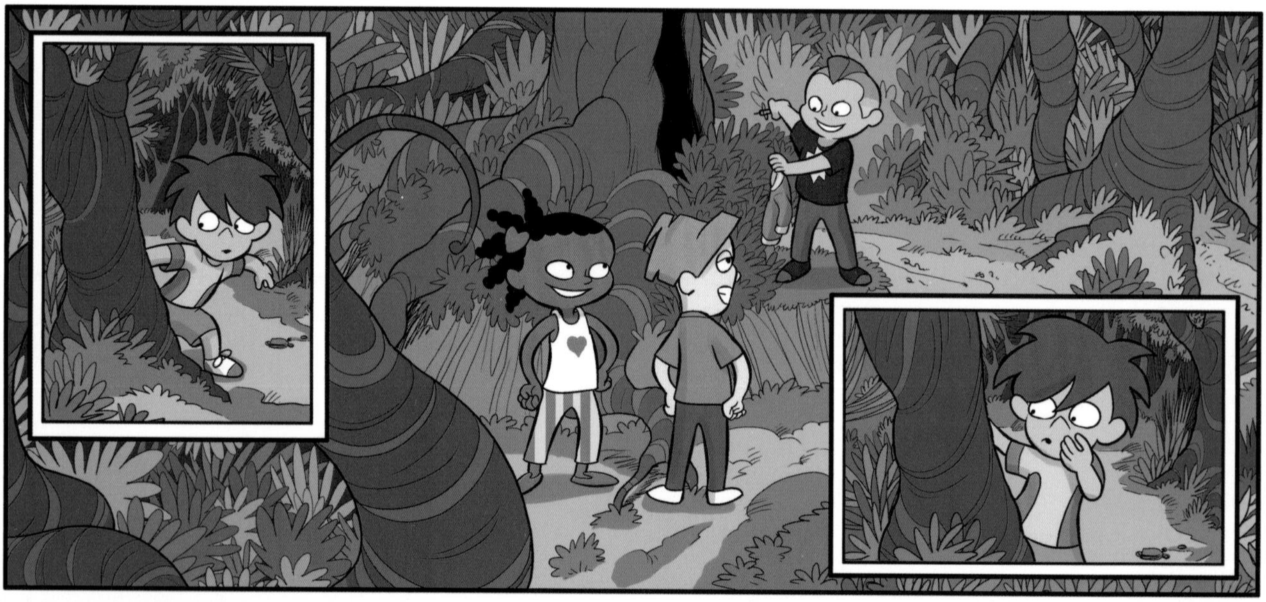

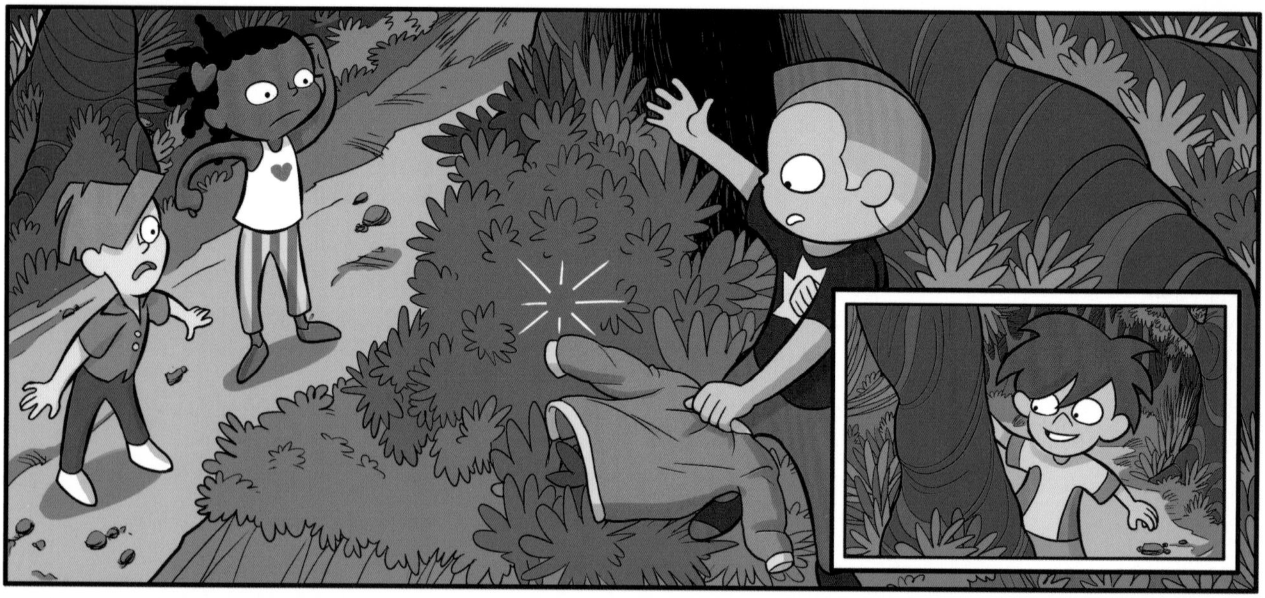

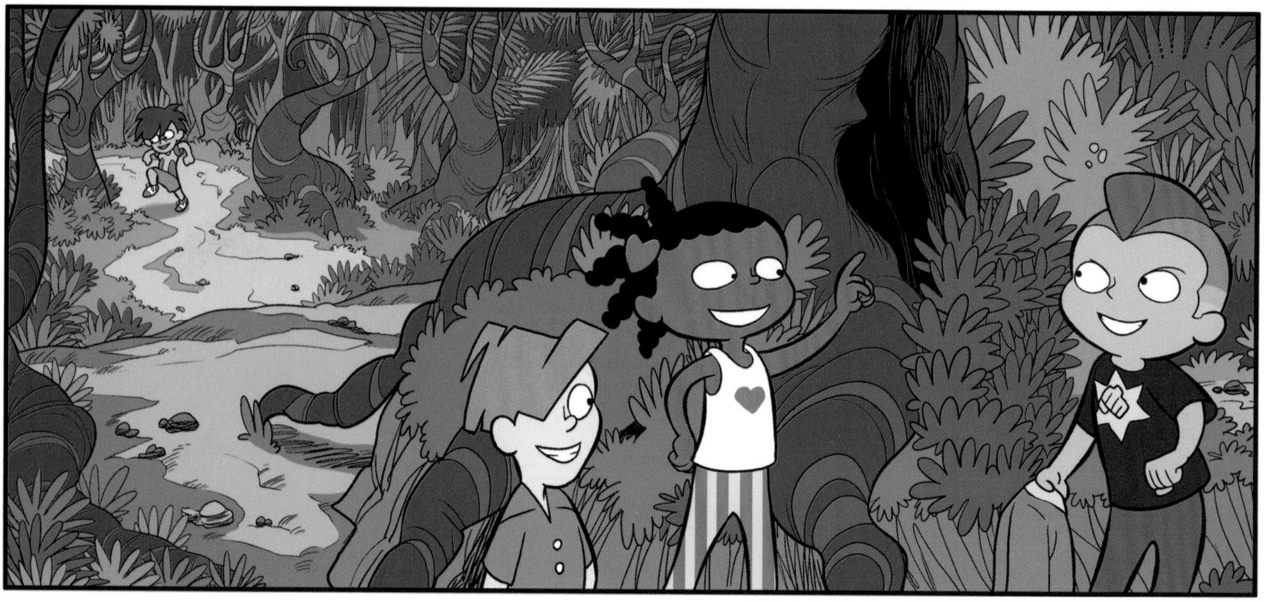

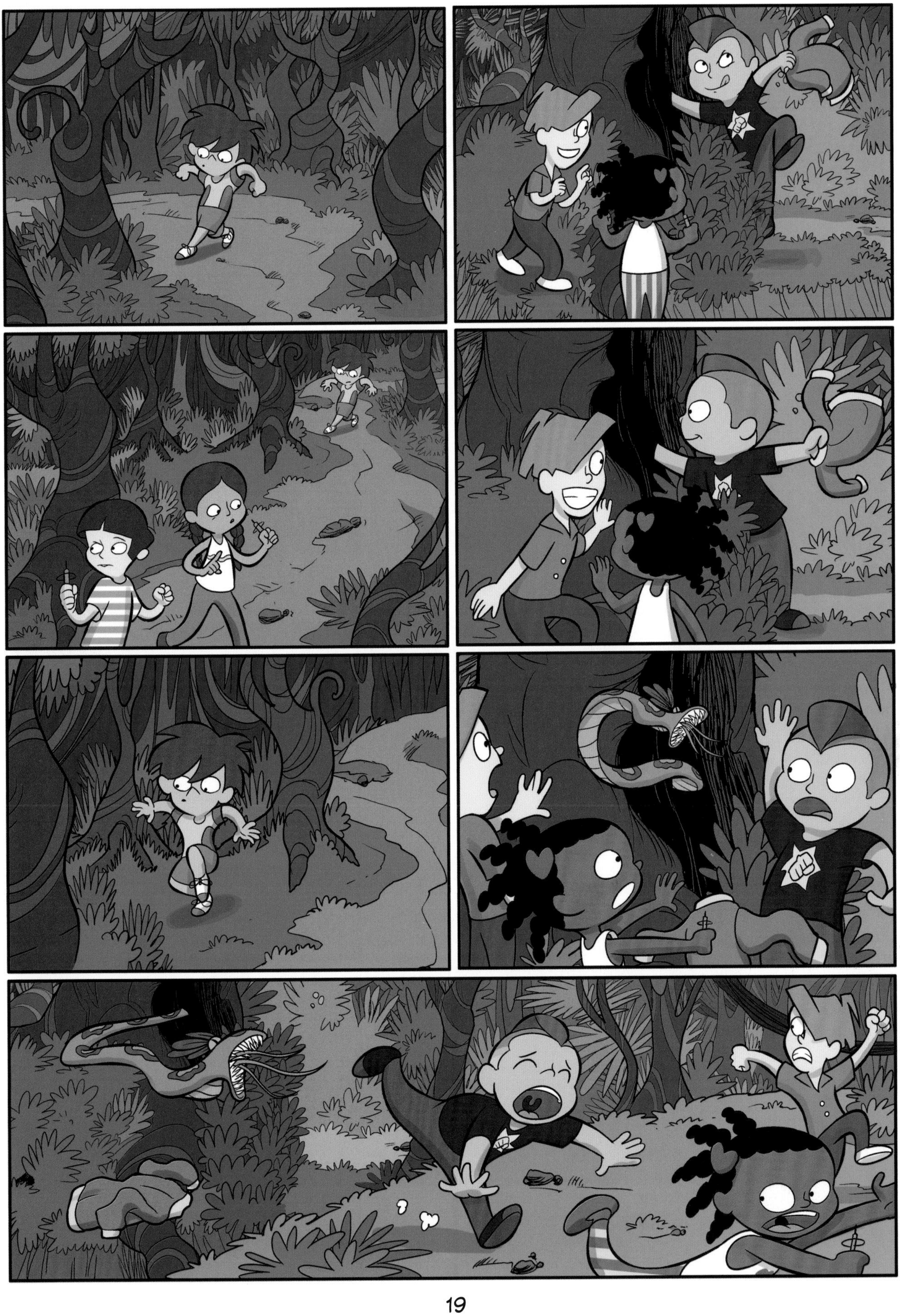

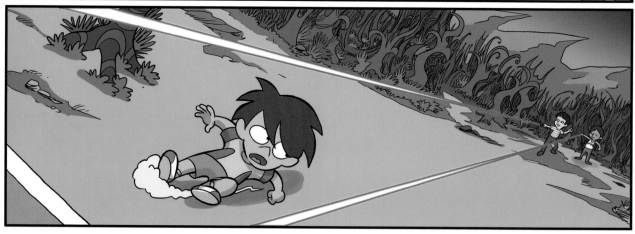

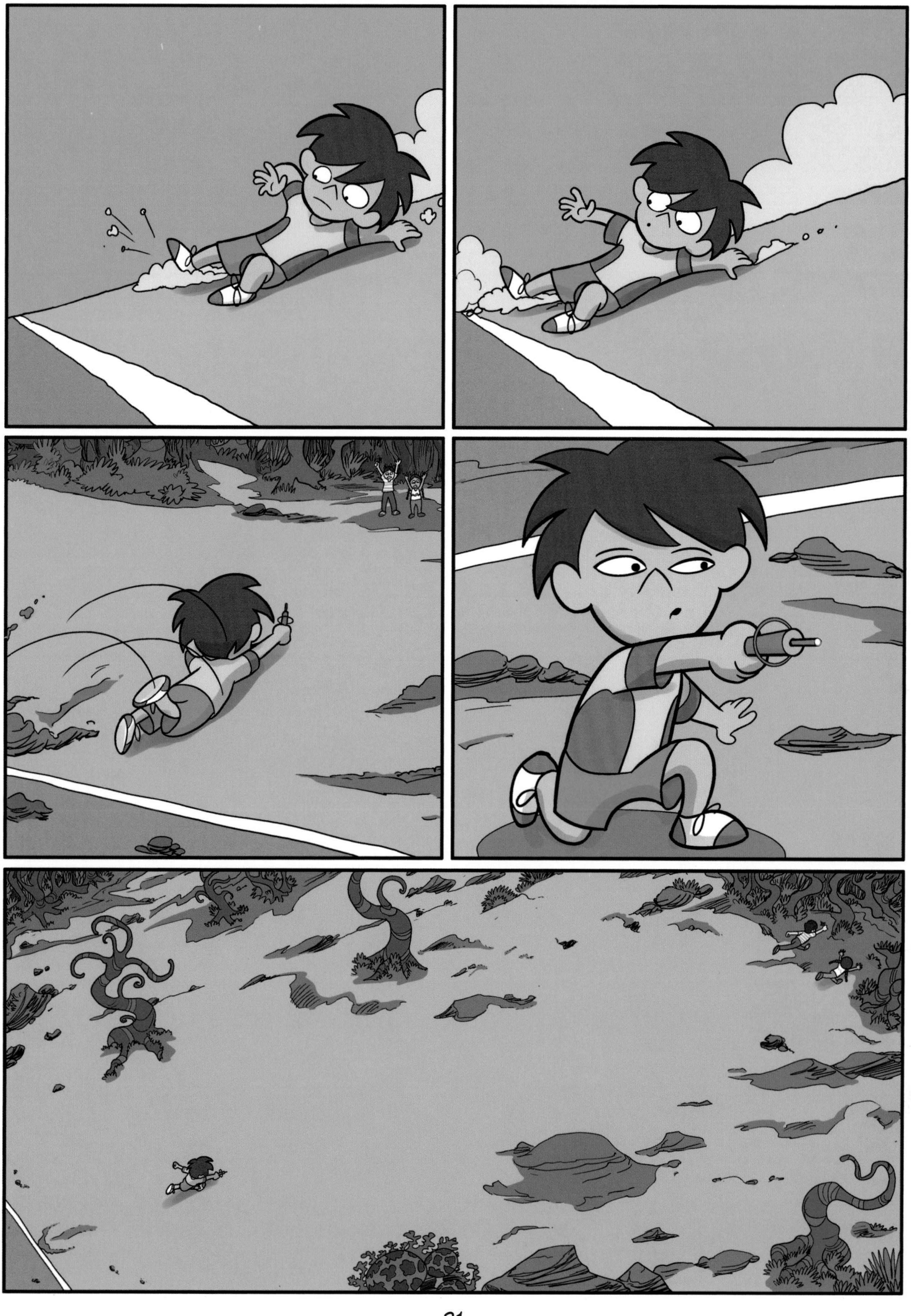

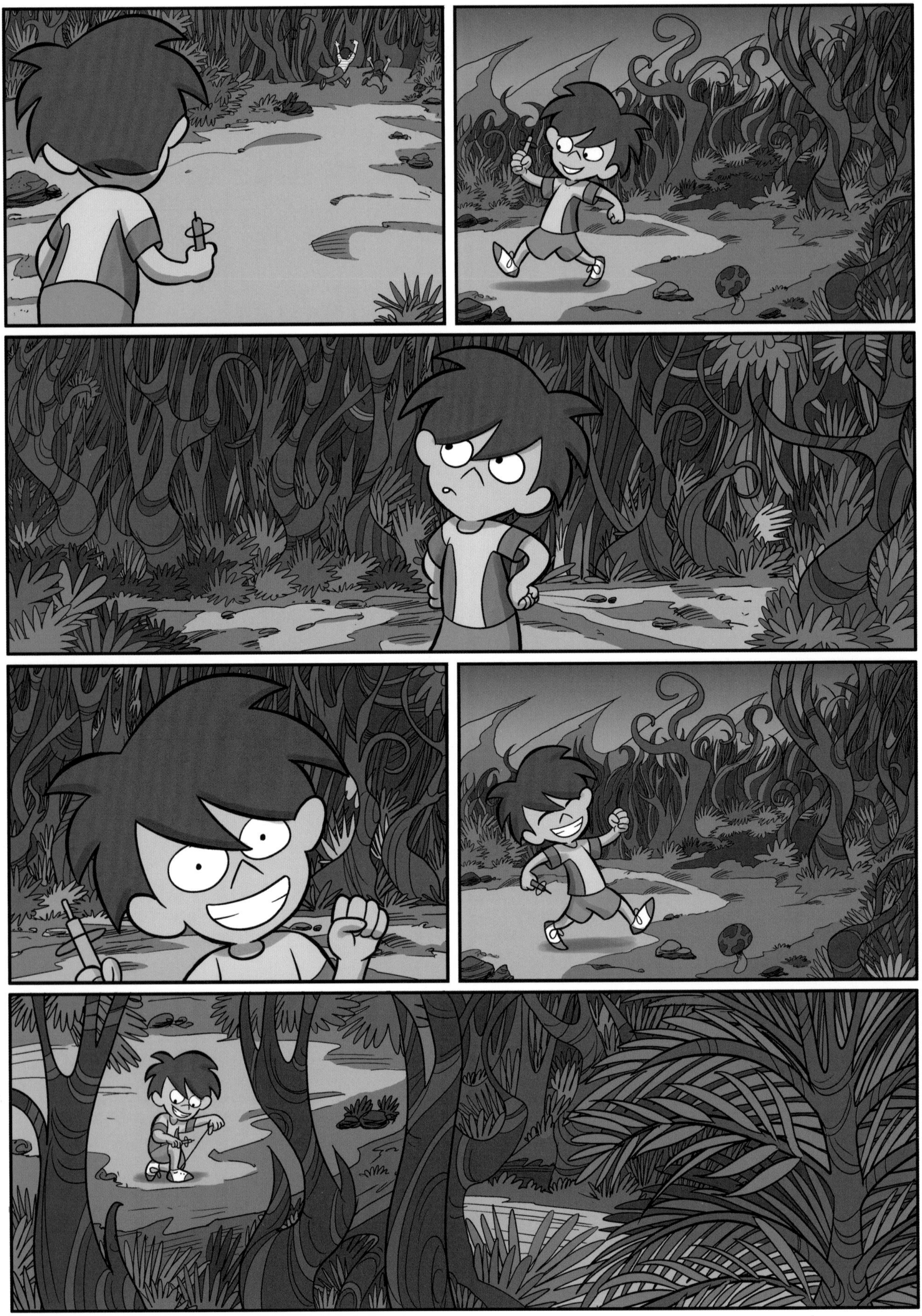

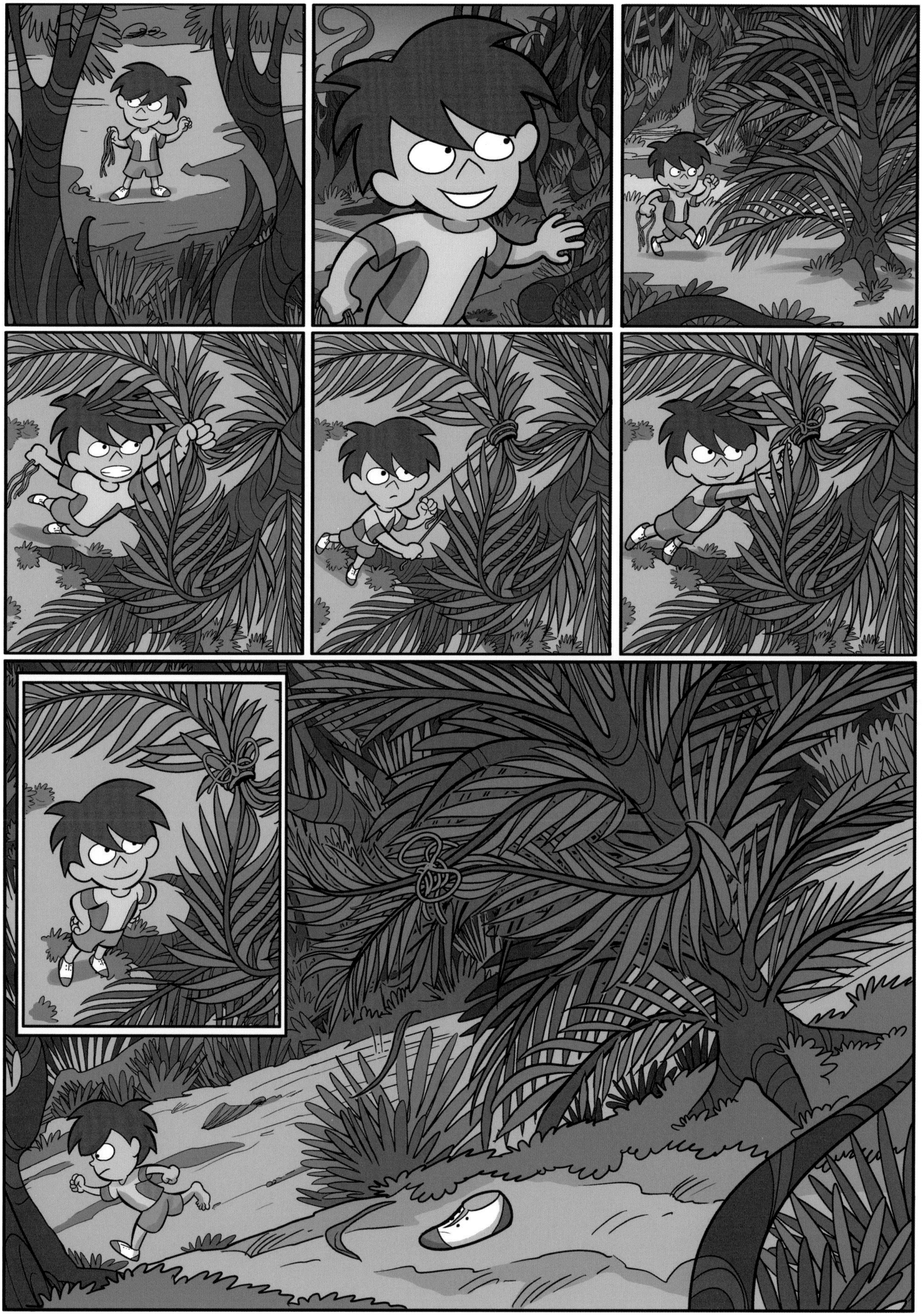

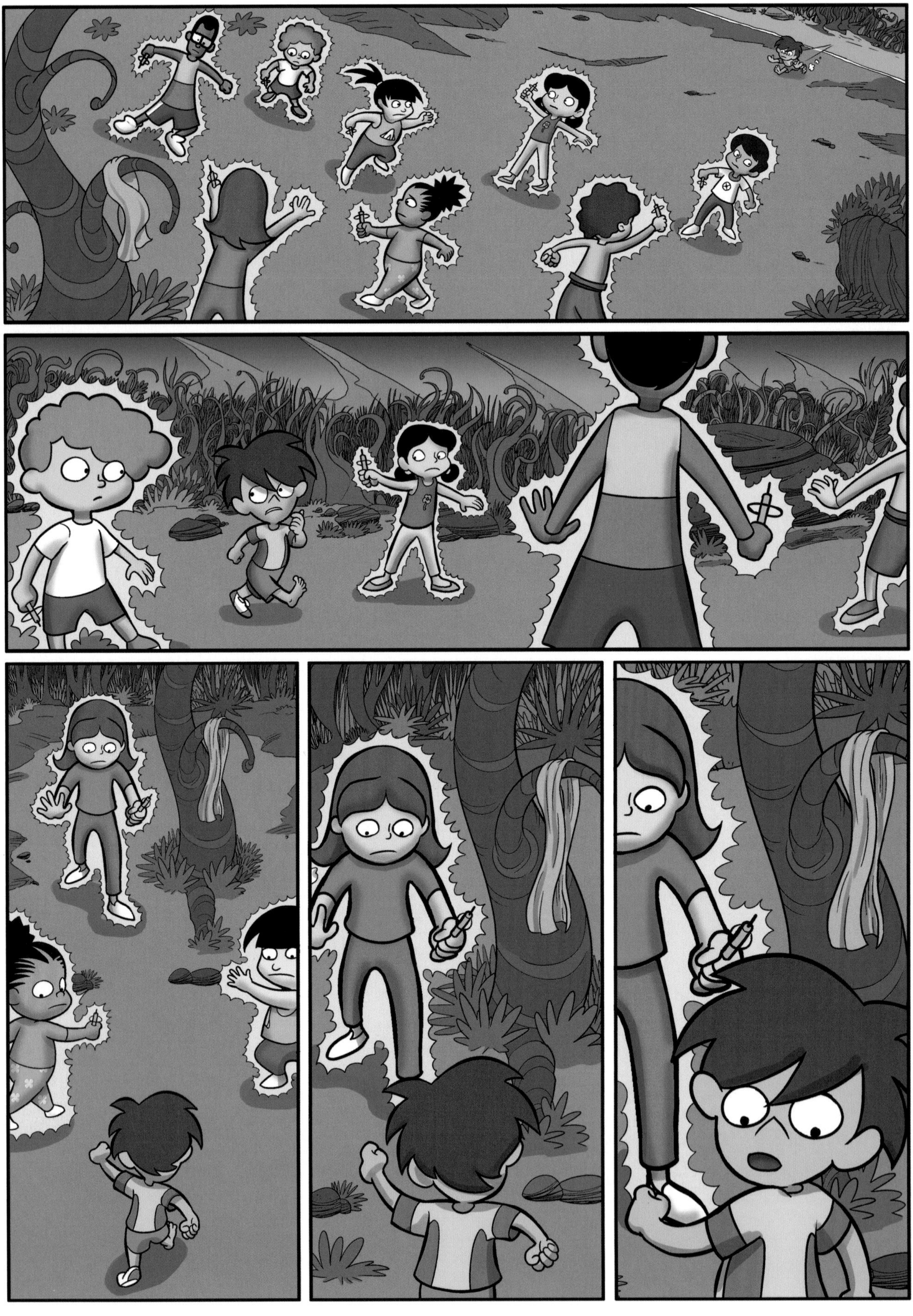

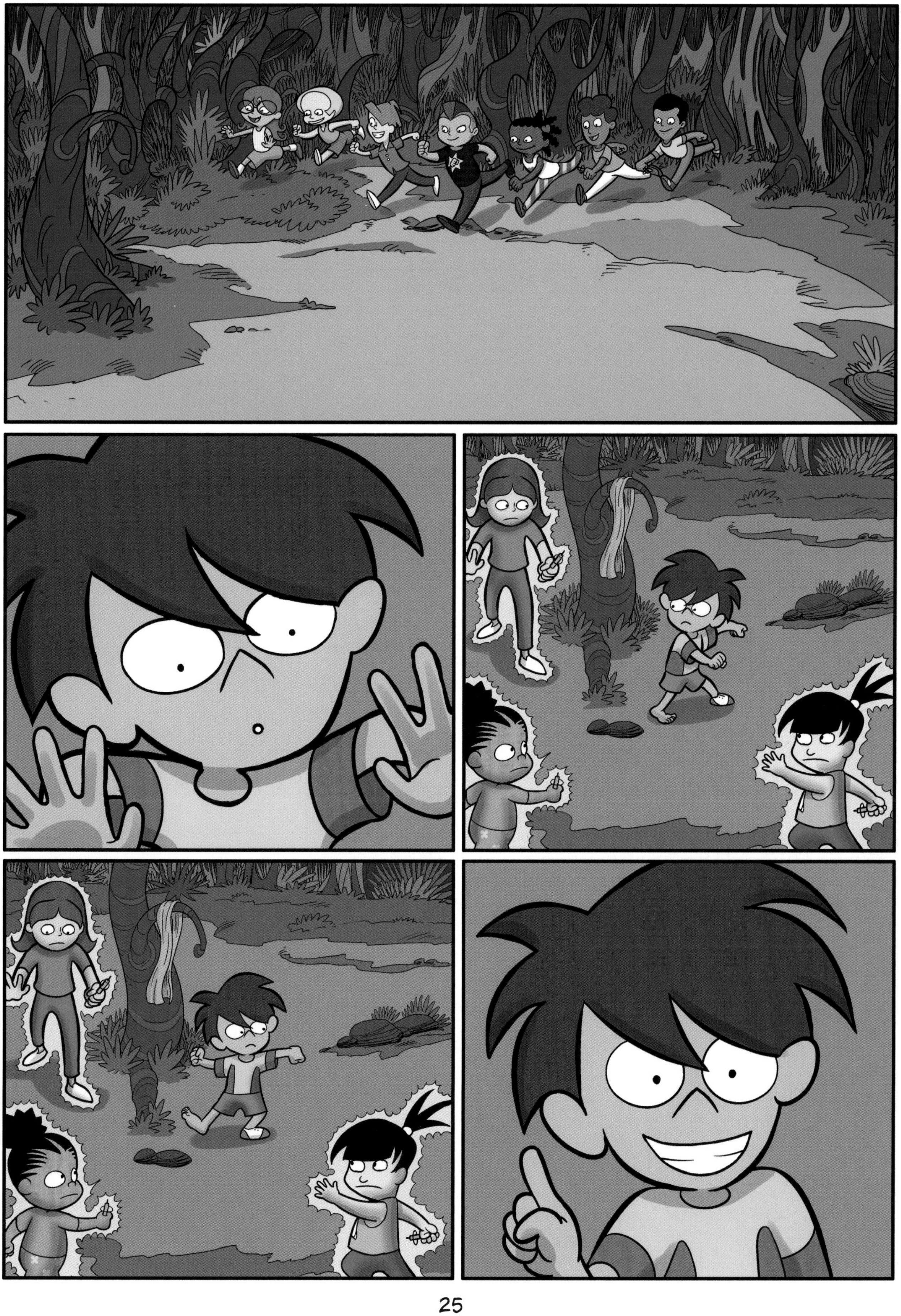

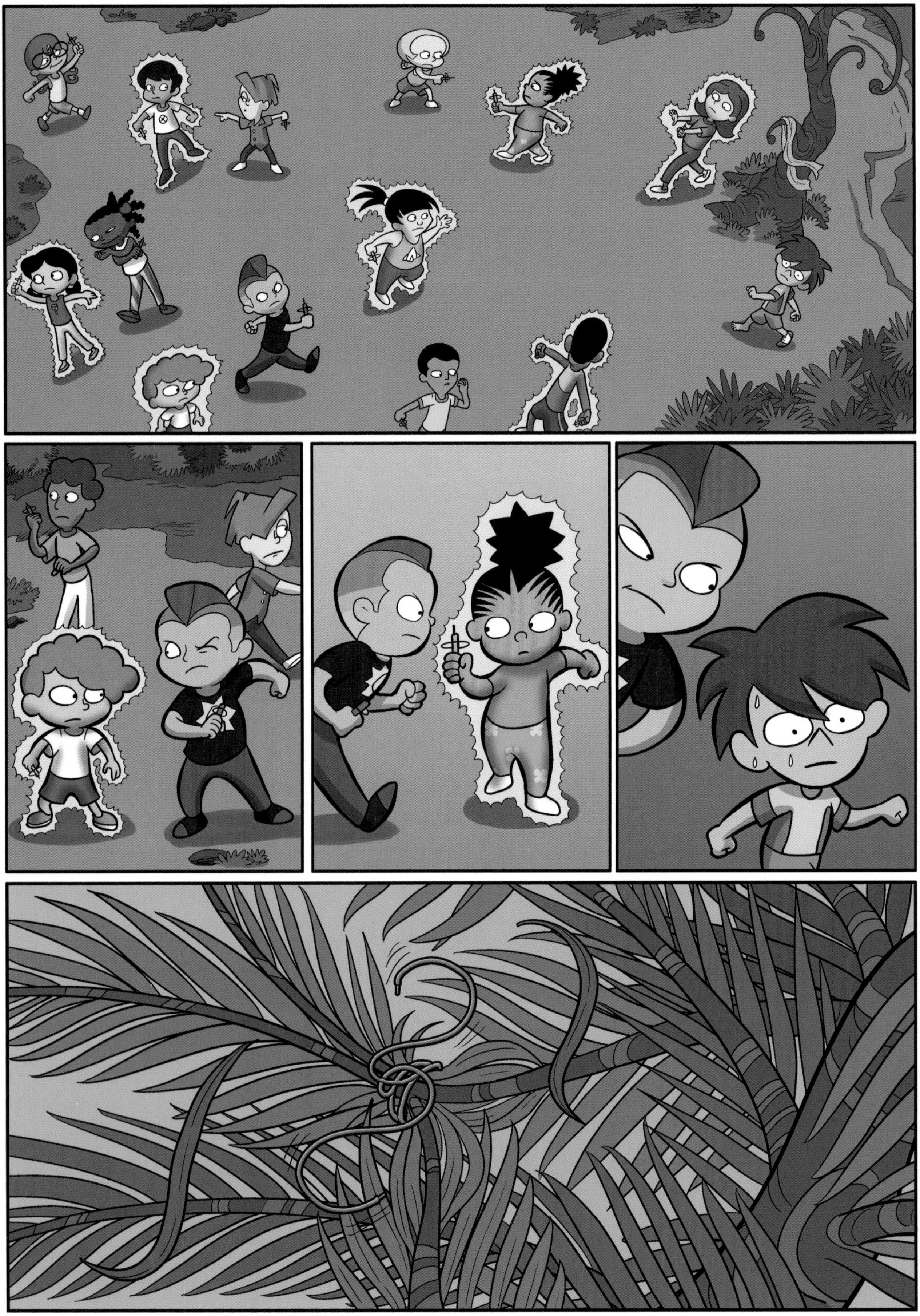

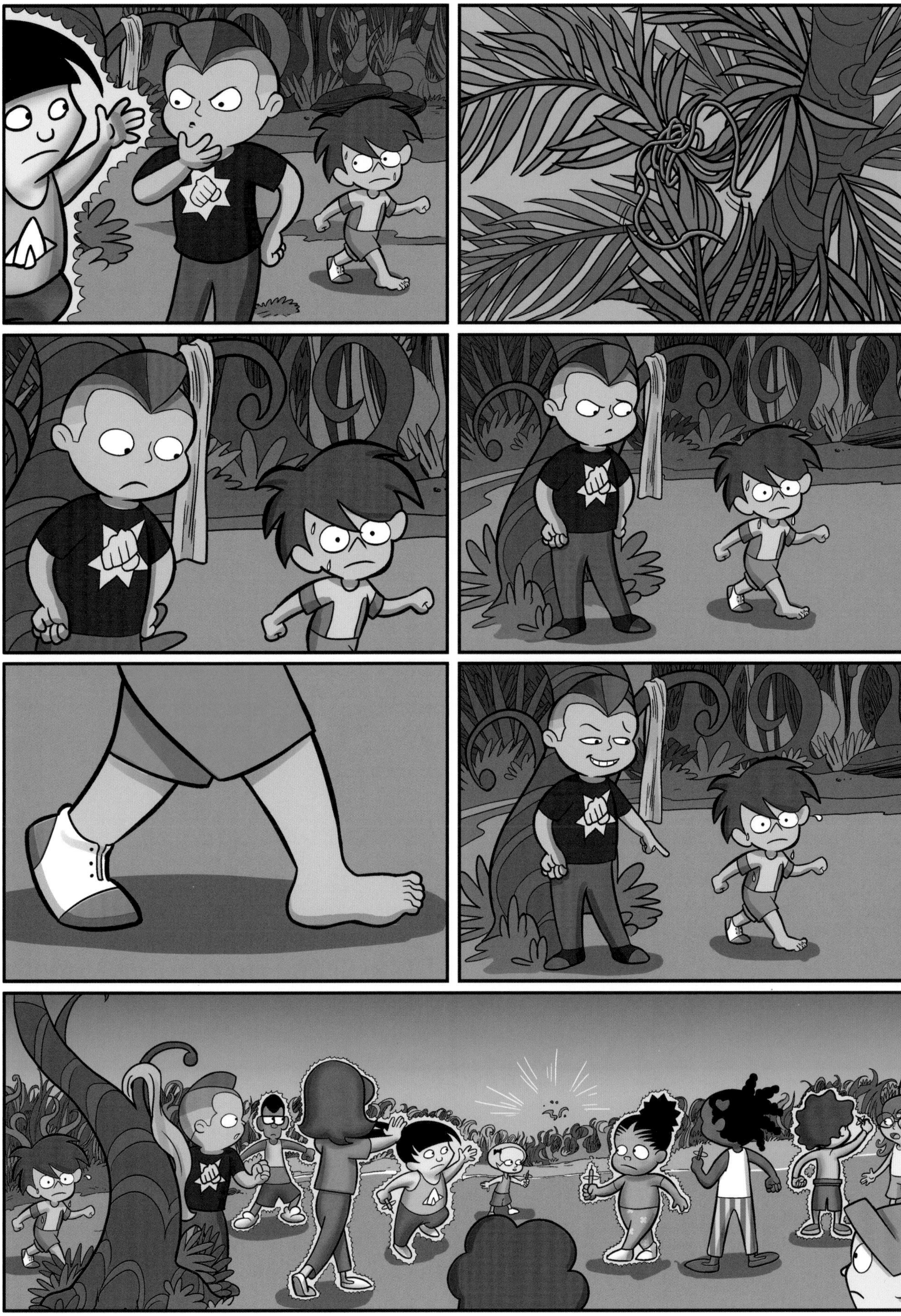

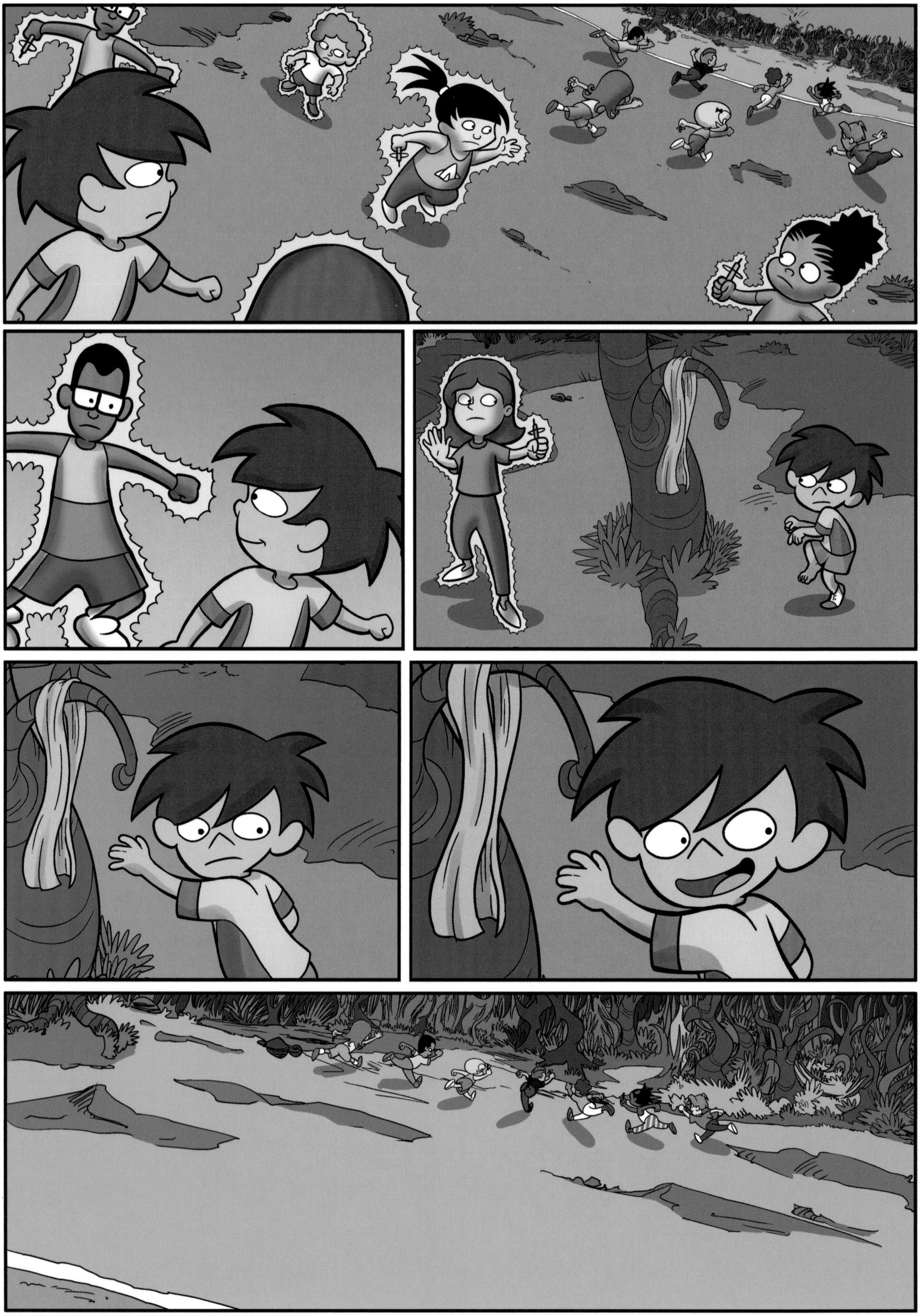

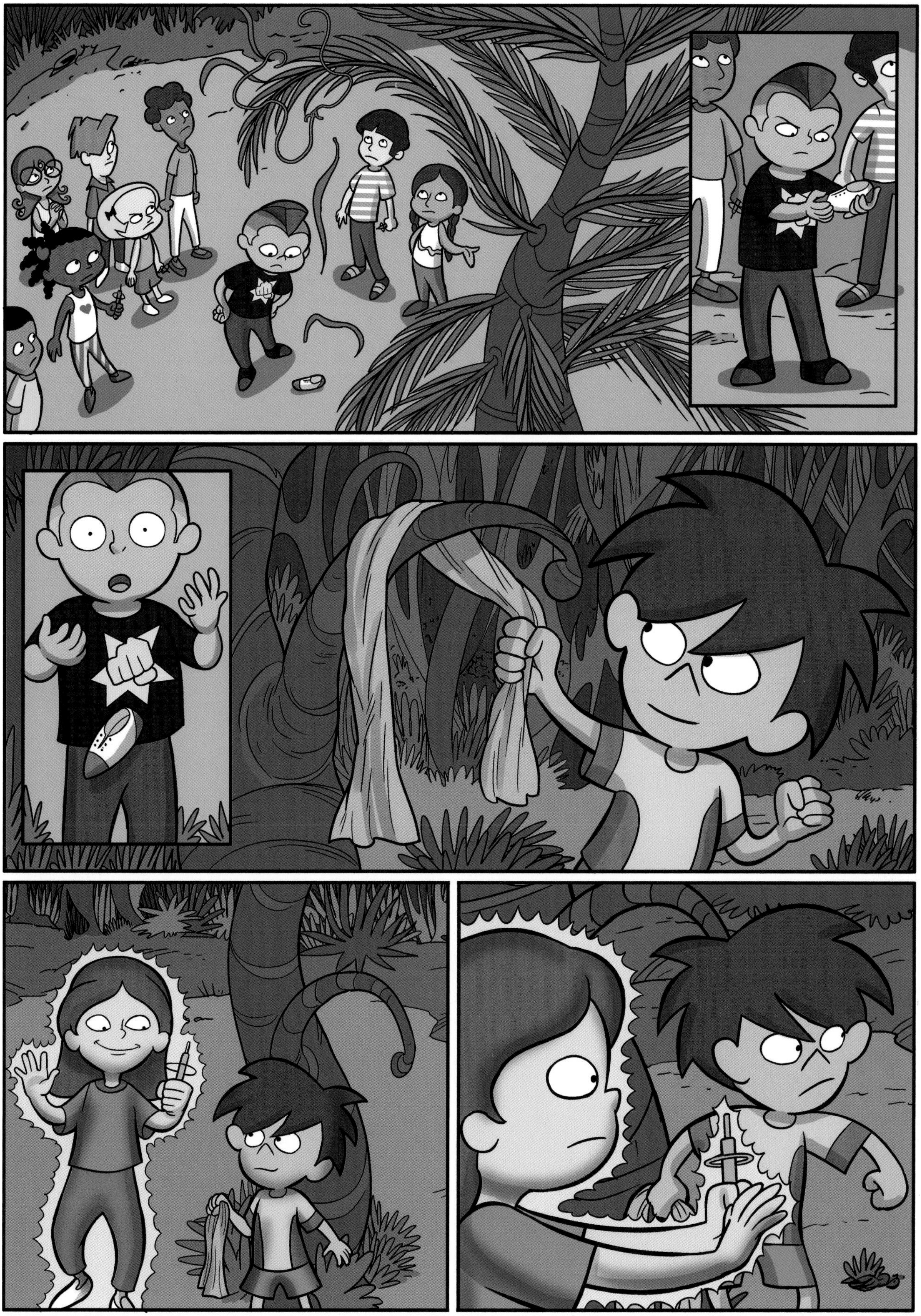

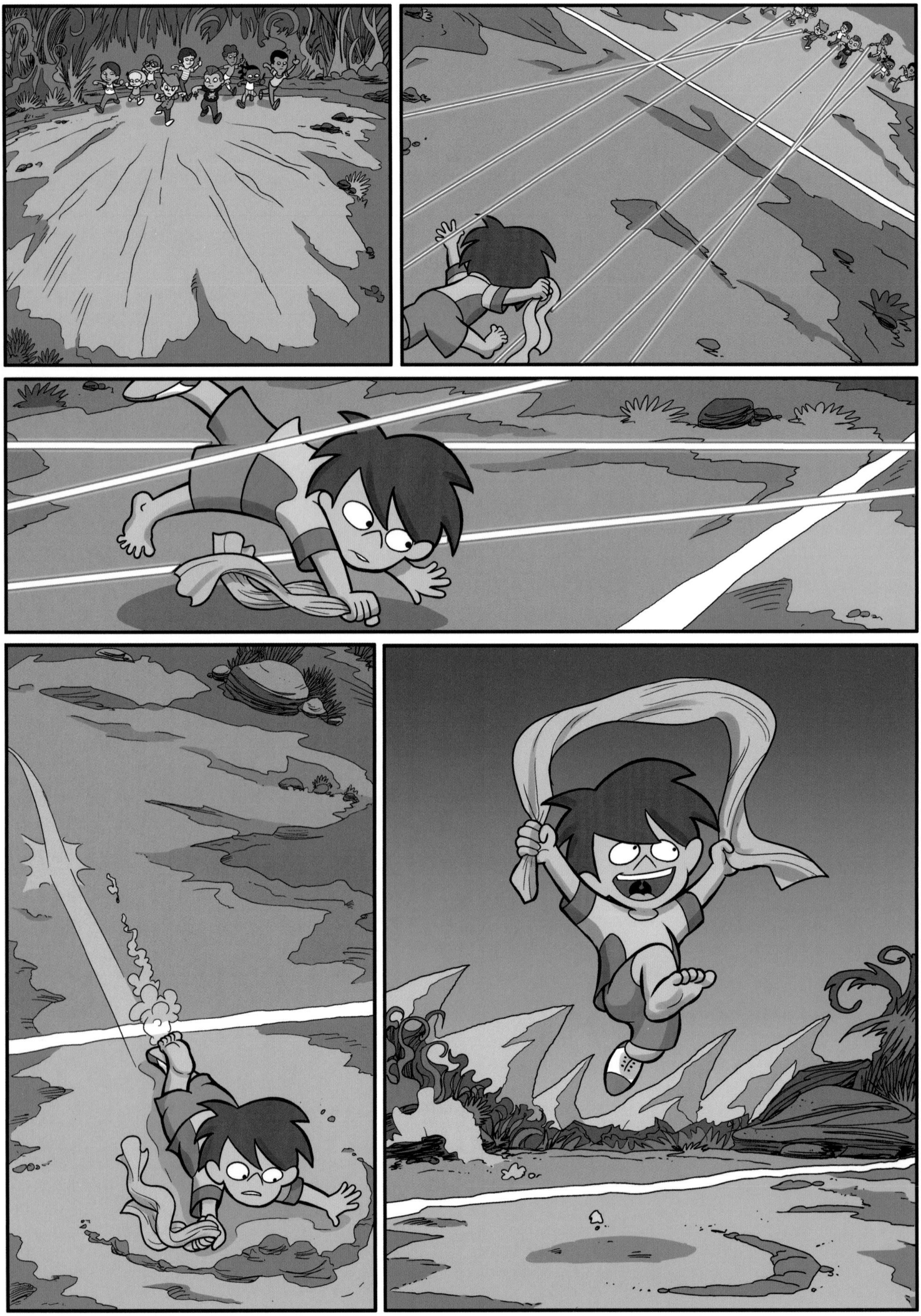

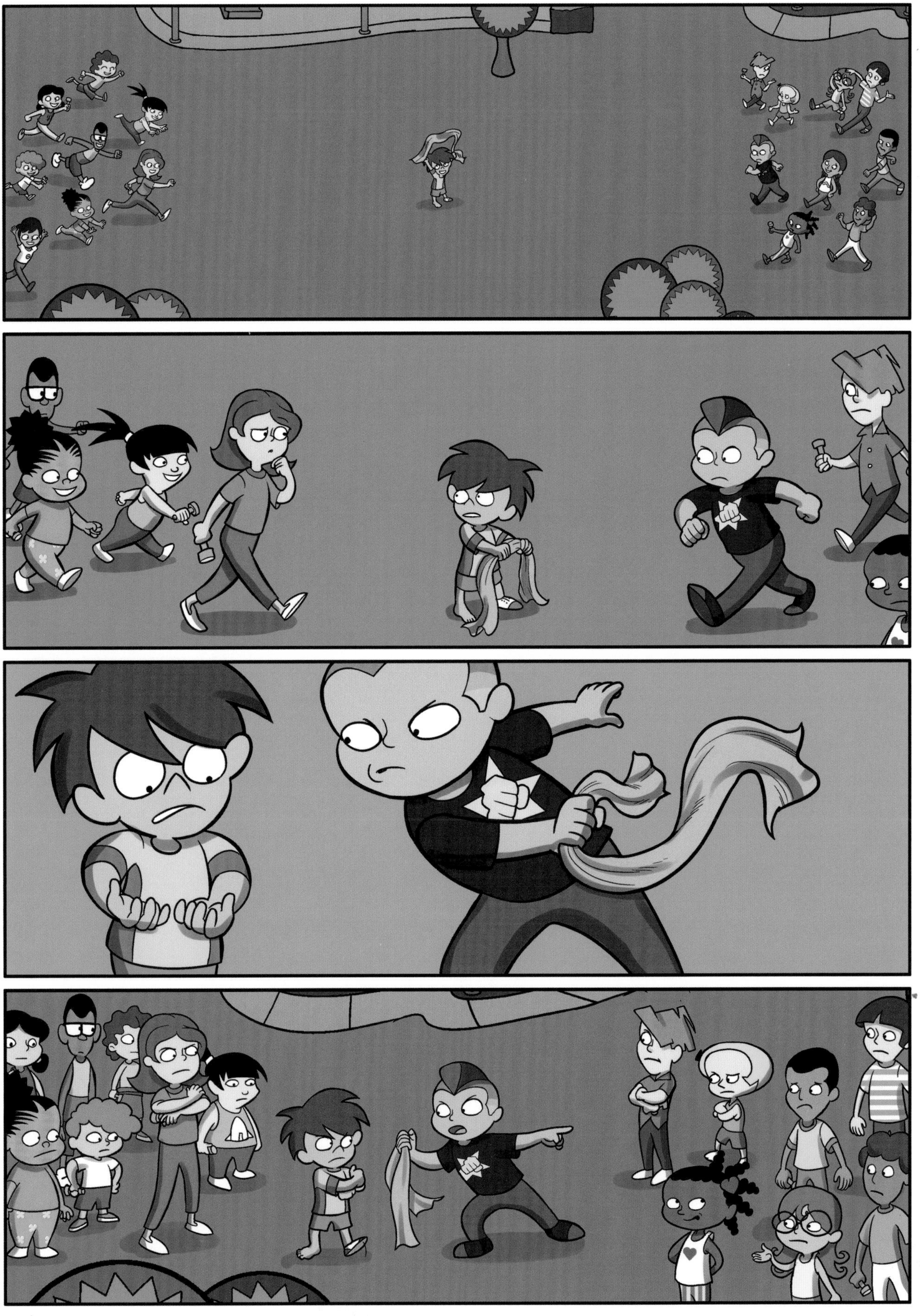

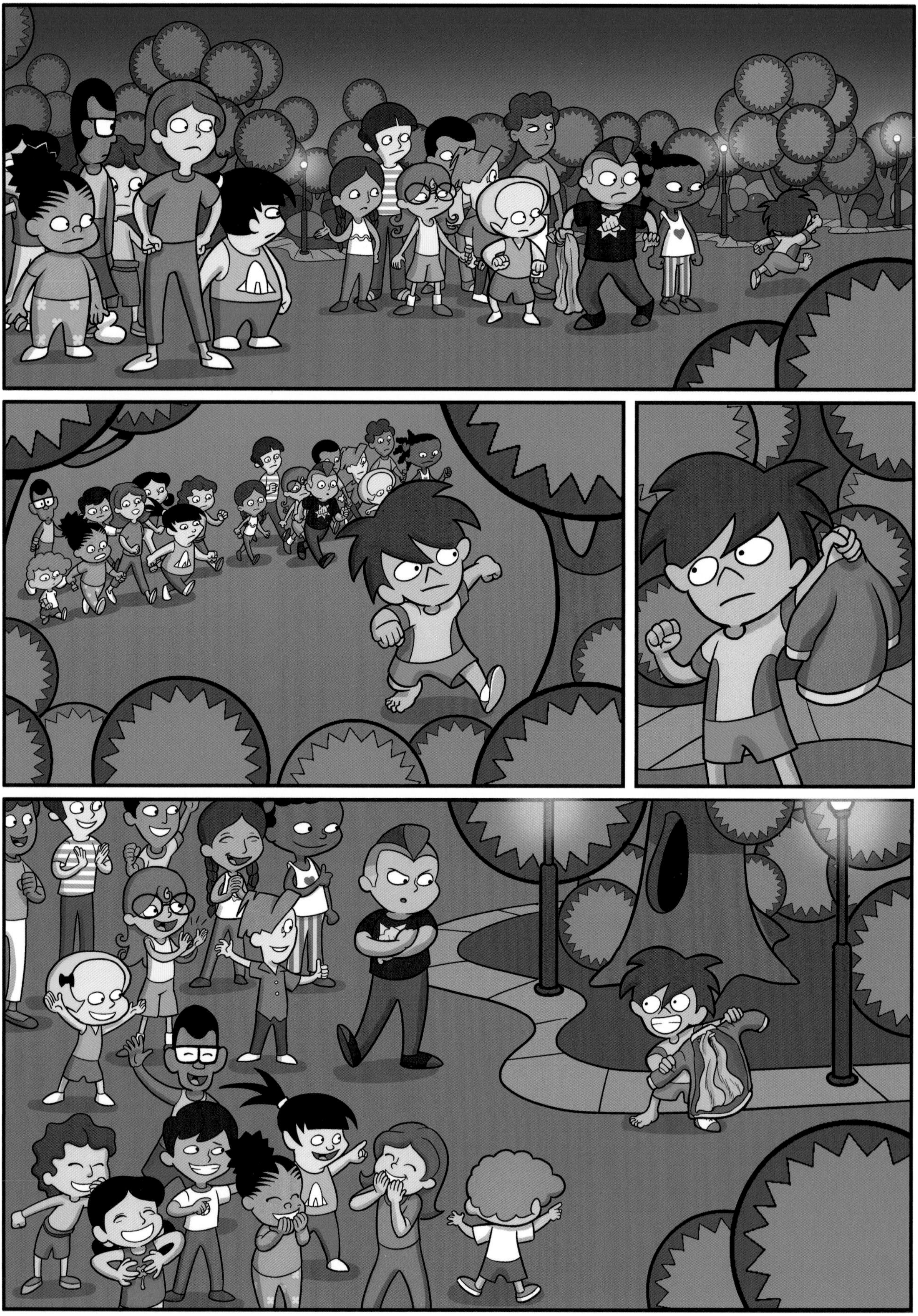

THE END

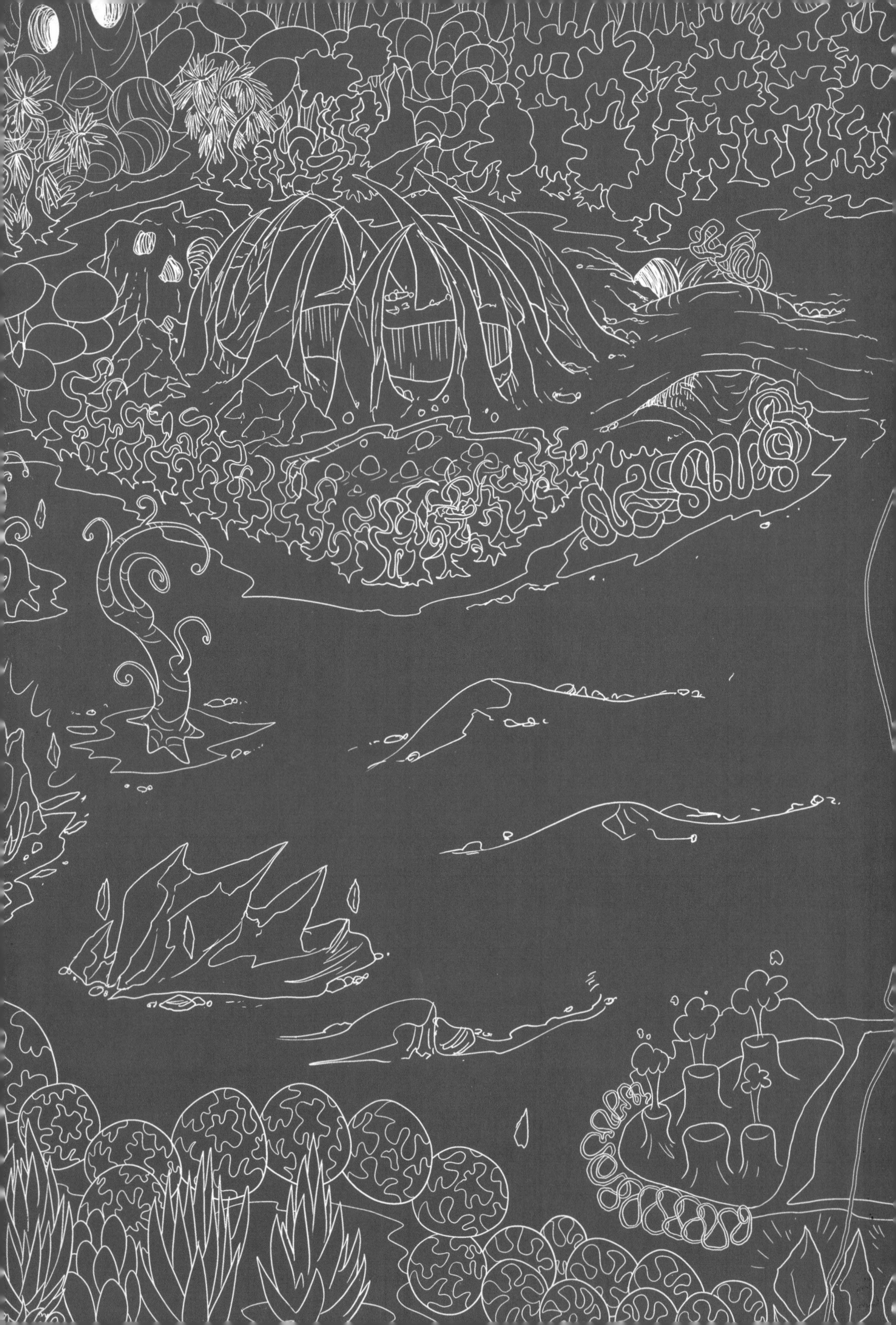